DATE DUE

DATE DUE

Fort Deception

Fort Deception

Cliff Farrell

THORNDIKE
CHIVERS

This Large Print edition is published by Thorndike Press®,
Waterville, Maine USA and by BBC Audiobooks, Ltd,
Bath, England.

Published in 2004 in the U.S. by arrangement with
Golden West Literary Agency.

Published in 2005 in the U.K. by arrangement with
Golden West Literary Agency.

U.S. Hardcover 0-7862-7121-3   (Western)
U.K. Hardcover 1-4056-3222-4   (Chivers Large Print)
U.K. Softcover 1-4056-3223-2   (Camden Large Print)

The text of this Large Print edition is unabridged.
Other aspects of the book may vary from the original edition.

Set in 16 pt. Plantin by Minnie B. Raven.

Printed in the United States on permanent paper.

British Library Cataloguing-in-Publication Data available

Library of Congress Cataloging-in-Publication Data

Farrell, Cliff.
    Fort Deception / by Cliff Farrell.
    p. cm.
    ISBN 0-7862-7121-3 (lg. print : hc : alk. paper)
    1. Fur traders — Fiction.   2. Trappers — Fiction.
I. Title.
PS3556.A766F37 2004
    813'.54—dc22   2004058823

Fort Deception

Many winters have rolled across the plains since the events that are set down herewith took place. Some say the plains have been conquered. But the vast distances have not dwindled. The buffalo are gone, but the cloud shadows drift in multitude across a land in which they lose themselves. The blizzards still blow unchecked, and men cower before them and sometimes die. And women too. It is in this land that such as Zachary Logan and Jeanne Fitzhugh met.

It was from the contents of a memory book that the story came to light. The book was found in a trunk made of buffalo leather that had lain for years in the dusty attic of an early-day mansion in St. Louis.

It had belonged to a great-great-aunt on the Fitzhugh side of the family. It contained old letters and pictures and yellowed clippings from newspapers. It had once fallen into the hands of Mandan Indians far up in the Dakota country, but had been recovered and completed later by its owner.

There were pages of narrative, set down while matters were still fresh in memory. Fortunately, Seraphine Clymena Fitzhugh, among her other accomplishments, possessed a talent for letting us see clearly in her memoirs just how it had been.

But let us start with some of the clippings:

(From the New York, N.Y.,
Evening Post, issue of July 6, 1833).

Departures!

Miss Seraphine Clymena Fitzhugh and her niece, Miss Jeanne Kathryn Fitzhugh, of the wealthy fur company family, were among the travelers who left by Jersey ferry this morning for Philadelphia. They will visit friends, no doubt. A pleasant journey, we say, and we trust that they will find the outlands not too unendurable during their stay, which we are sure will be short. (Philadelphia papers please take note.)

(From the *Pennsylvania Packet,*
Philadelphia, Pa., issue of July 8,1833)

Departures!

The westward tide grows. The steam
train leaving by way of the cable
railway for the mountain country this
morning was crowded beyond sane
capacity. Many passengers preferred to
risk their necks by riding on the roofs
rather than suffer being packed like
sheep inside the cars.

We noticed two rather well-dressed
ladies jammed in a car among motley
humanity. One was young, the other
more mature. Beyond vouchsafing that
their names were Smith they avoided
further information, except to admit
that they were bound for the western
reaches of the state. Accompanying
them was a natty, middle-aged gen-
tleman who curtly refused to answer
our queries. Fine-feathered emigrants,
we say.

Beneath this excerpt, Seraphine Fitzhugh had penned this comment: "A very
impertinent young man, but typical of
these uncultured Philadelphians. I regret

that I let Jeanne answer any of his questions."

(From the Pittsburgh, Pa.,
Gazette, issue of July 16,1833)

Departures!

The packet *River Gem*, which brought cargo from St. Louis of hides, smoked buffalo tongue, ginseng and tallow, will leave tonight after being delayed two days by the necessity of repairing a steam box. It will carry mainly flour, pig lead, barreled whiskey and bottled porter. Among the passengers are two members of the fair sex who complained bitterly to the captain because the odor of buffalo hides lingers on the *River Gem*. But to no avail. The ladies are listed as Miss Sarah Smith and Miss Jeanne Smith, the latter being the younger. They appeared very refined and we can only "fancy" what might be the purpose of their trip to the Mississippi port. In their company was a surly person who declared that his name was Samuel Hunter.

Beneath this, Seraphine Fitzhugh had written: "So now we're labeled as fancy ladies. I'll be socially ruined. And Jeanne also, but she doesn't seem to give a tinker. Her father would turn over in his grave if he knew about this fantastic venture. Sam Hunter, reading this over my shoulder, says her grandfather and great-grandfather would do the same. True. Too true."

(From the *Missouri Gazette*, St. Louis, Mo., issue of July 30, 1833)

Departures!

A Fitzhugh Fur Company keelboat, which has been renamed the Jeanne Kathryn Fitzhugh, will leave at four o'clock ante meridian tomorrow, bound for Fort Jeanne on the plains. The reader will note that both the craft and the fort bear a name which honors some fair member of the famous old fur family of which J. K. Fitzhugh is the head. A beautiful name, say we.

And (please whisper this) rumors are rife that the lady herself is in St. Louis in person under a *nom de guerre*. Furthermore it is said that she and a chaperon are to be passengers on the keelboat for the trip to the trading post which was named for her when she was born. Such gossip is not to be believed. No white woman has ever gone into the mountains to our knowledge, and certainly none by keelboat.

However, it is a fact that the boat was made ready rather hurriedly for the journey. Its captain, Doughbelly Biggle, is worried about whether his craft will make it to Fort Jeanne before winter sets in. He has cause for concern, say we. We bid him *bon voyage,* and trust that he does not suffer indigestion from an Indian arrow en route.

Seraphine Fitzhugh's comment to this: "Well, at last we're really on our way, heading up the Mississippi River toward the mouth of the Missouri with a whole horde of hairy, ugly, impudent rascals who call themselves *voyageurs* pushing this ungainly craft along by using long poles. Captain Biggle tells us we will not reach our destination until late October, and then only if everything goes well.

Jeanne is wondering what it will be like in this wild country so far away. I imagine we will know eventually, to our regret."

CHAPTER ONE

Squaw winter had come and gone in the upper Missouri River country. Its frosts had painted blazing hues of butter yellow and vermilion on the alder and willows and plum brush. The blue haze of Indian summer now lay like velvet over the land, lulling the mind to the knowledge that this was but an interlude.

It was a time for dreaming, a time for release of the spirit. A man could believe that his strength was tenfold, and, because he could not help it, Zack Logan arose from beside the cookfire where he had been lolling, talking to his friends, laid aside his pipe, and lifted a weighty length of waterlogged cottonwood trunk which had drifted aground nearby.

The log was heavier than he had anticipated, but he welcomed the challenge. Sinews tightened and back muscles ridged. Strong legs, his shanks bare well above his moccasins, in tattered, shrunken buckskin breeches, stood braced. He was taller than most men and brawnier. His hair was dark and thick, and he had not had an opportunity to shave in days. His chin was forceful, with a nose to match, and both of these features had collided violently with eventful matters of life along the way, by the scars.

He balanced his burden, advanced a few strides, and, with a grunt, sent it whirling end over end into the river. He grinned, pleased that his faith in himself had been justified but a little abashed at making such a display.

There were five onlookers. One was Belzey Williams, a lantern-jawed, sun-cured lodgepole of a man. Thanks to the industry of his two Crow wives who were busy at the moment at the cookfire, Belzey was smartly arrayed in a new hunting shirt, fringed breeches, and white, high-topped moccasins.

"Better save your gristle for fendin' that raft o' yours off the rock chains downriver, old hoss," Belzey advised. "It's a mighty long float from here to St. Louis, an' there'll be snow flyin' before you raise the mouth o' the Kaw, or this child's a possum."

"Today," said Zack, "it will take more than weather to bother me. It's downhill from here on. I feel so good I might sprout wings and fly."

Another spectator was the missionary, the Rev. Angus Macleod, whose work had made him known and respected among the plains tribes to the south and tolerated even by the testy Utes. His assistant was a baptized, aged Pawnee who carried both a crows-foot charm in a medicine sack and a prayer book on thongs around his neck as double insurance against misfortune.

Angus Macleod was tossing snacks of meat to a highbred, gentlemanly, Scottish staghound. The dog, magnificent in size and in the prime of health, had eyes and affection only for his master.

"A bra' fine boy ye are, MacDuff," Angus said.

Because of the warmth of the afternoon the missionary had laid aside his rusty black frock coat and his shirt. He wore only buckskin breeches and moccasins. Zack noted approvingly that these were nearly as ragged as his own. Here was a humble man who followed the call of God on his own two feet.

Angus Macleod was also big enough to wrestle the devil in person, almost as big as Zack himself. At sixty, Angus's shoulders were blacksmith-broad and plated with muscle. A mane of gray hair framed craggy features. His Scot blue eyes were softened by a tolerance of mankind's weaknesses.

He strode to the river's margin and retrieved the log which had floated ashore.
Hoisting it aloft, he hurled it in an attempt
to match Zack's effort. But it fell short.

"Bah!" he snorted. "I am growing soft."
He fetched Zack a staggering slap on the
back. "Would that I could take ye to
Aberdeen, Zachary, and teach ye to speak
with a burr of heather in your voice so that
ye could pose as a Macleod. Ye would hu-
miliate the arrogant McGregor clan at
their own game of tossing the caber, a
sport at which they practiced day and
night so that they would have some little
item to crow about over us Macleods."

"I've heard of the caber toss," Zack said.
"But I'd prefer to throw something a little
more worth while."

Angus eyed him shrewdly. "A certain
person named Quinn Spain, perhaps?"

"Or J. K. Fitzhugh," Zack said.

"I have been told that Fitzhugh Fur
treated ye and your brother rather rough,"
Angus said.

Zack turned and looked at him. "Rough?
That's like calling a tiger a tabby cat! A
weak word for murder, Reverend!"

"Murder? Ye must mean your brother's
death. But, lad, I understood that Daniel

was lost in the river. Drowned."

"On a keelboat that was cut adrift at night so that it would be wrecked on a rock chain in rough water," Zack said. "Dan couldn't swim. He wasn't the only one. Three other Logan men drowned too."

"An accident."

"The mooring lines were slashed," Zack said.

"Now, Zachary! How can ye know that? Ye were not there."

"I got the truth out of a Fitzhugh *voyageur*. He named the man who did it. Jules Lebow. He's Spain's bootlicker."

"By what means did ye get the truth, as ye call it, out of this man?" Angus asked uneasily.

"With my hands," Zack said. "With my hands on his gullet. I let him live. I was that soft, for he was in on the wreck of Dan's boat."

"God forgive ye, lad," Angus sighed. "A poor wretch might say anything under such circumstances. Ye know that."

"What about tying men to trees and using a whip on their backs?" Zack demanded.

"What are ye saying?"

Zack nodded to Belzey. The mountain man peeled off his hunting shirt. Angus

18

Macleod stared at the pale, long-healed scars that stood out on Belzey's back.

"Belzey was a Logan trapper," Zack said. "It was Jules Lebow who swung the whip on him. Ten and one lashes in the stockade at Fort Jeanne in the presence of Mandan and Ree and Nez Percé chiefs who were called in to be impressed by the power of Fitzhugh Fur. This was right after Dan died in the river. Quinn Spain couldn't get his hands on me so he grabbed Belzey and used him as an example of what would happen to me when they caught me."

"It's impossible," Angus said. But he was now uncertain.

Belzey uttered a snort. "Spoken like a pulpit-pounder what couldn't see daylight between a mule's ears."

"I assure ye I will pound the pulpit and preach against such sinners as ye, Belzey Williams," Angus said. "For shame! Two wives! Ye will be punished in the hereafter unless ye mend your ways and repent."

Belzey pulled on his shirt. "A man's got a right to live in a warm lodge," he said complacently. "Leastwise, I won't be alone if I'm punished in the happy land. Some o' them old codgers from Scriptures will ketch it too along with me, from what I've heerd o' their carryin's on."

" 'Tis possible those scars on your back are already part of your punishment," Angus said.

"Maybe so," Belzey replied. "Maybe not. No matter. All I know is thet they were put there in the name o' J. K. Fitzhugh. I ain't sayin' he was there in person. He keeps his hide safe an' unstretched a long way from the mountains. He knows there're men like me who'd put a ball in his lights quicker'n I could scalp a Digger. It was Quinn Spain who passed sentence an' read the order in J. K. Fitzhugh's name. I've been waitin' all these three years for a chance to twist a knife in the ribs of either one, but even Spain has kept out of my way."

"If there's been injustice then vengeance is not for ye to take, Belzey," Angus said earnestly. "Nor ye, Zachary."

Zack looked at the missionary with wintry eyes. He became thoughtful, running a hand reflectively over the silky black beard that gave him a piratical aspect. His hand was big, the knuckles prominent and very hard.

His weight was normally around one hundred and ninety pounds, balanced on a strong-boned frame. He was probably ten pounds lighter at the moment, but he was all sinew and pliable muscle.

He was thinking of his back trail. In June he had been within sight of the great greenrollers from the open Pacific, watching them break on the western coast near where the Columbia River merged with salt water. In July he had been afoot and on thin rations in the Bitterroot Valley after the crossing of the snow-drowned mountains. Three times he had crossed and recrossed the Bitterroot range, for he had lost all but one of his packhorses to thieving Flatheads on the far side, and had helped carry packs of furs on his own shoulders in relays over the passes.

He had bartered precious furs for ponies from the Nez Percé, and had evaded the Blackfoot until he had passed the falls of the Missouri. There he had abandoned the horses and built a raft on which he had floated hundreds of miles on the river as it coursed through the open plains.

"No preaching will change me, Reverend," he said. "It was only three years ago that Fitzhugh Fur smashed Logan Brothers, when Dan and myself tried to come into the mountains and compete with them. I'm only twenty-eight now, but I'm older than that. Three years like that ages a man."

"And hardens him," Angus sighed.

Zack shrugged. "I'm back, and with another stake to revive Logan Brothers Fur. This time I'll know how to deal with J. K. Fitzhugh and men like Quinn Spain."

He added, "Dan was too easygoing. Like yourself, he believed in the decency of men."

"And ye do not?" Angus challenged.

"You saw the scars on Belzey," Zack said.

He watched the missionary and Belzey glance dubiously at his small raft which was drawn up at water's edge. It was built of driftwood, bound together with lacings of willow withes and sinews of deer and buffalo.

Zack had appeared on it half an hour earlier, floating down the river, using an improvised sweep. The meeting with Belzey had been prearranged. Zack had encountered a party of trappers more than a week earlier upriver who knew Belzey's whereabouts. They had said Belzey was preparing to head out of the mountains for the winter. Belzey was the one person Zack could trust to bring him up to date on news of the trapping country, particularly as to the activities of Fitzhugh Fur.

He had sent word that he would meet Belzey at this spot which was mutually known to them. As it turned out, Belzey had arrived at the rendezvous a day ahead of him and had camped, awaiting his appearance by water.

Angus Macleod's presence was a matter of chance. The missionary had spent a summer of toil among the Gros Ventre in the Wind River country and was now on his way to a destination on the Missouri for the winter. He had come upon Belzey's camp an hour or two before the raft's arrival and had decided to stop there overnight, for he and Belzey were old friends despite their opposing views on secular matters.

Zack was well acquainted with the missionary also. Angus had for years carried on his work among the tribes along the upper Mississippi, preaching to the Sac and Fox, as well as to the Kaw and Pawnee of the middle border. He had often made his headquarters in St. Louis where he was known and respected by trappers and fur traders.

His board of missions in New York had finally sent him into the virgin and more dangerous fields among the savage horse Indians of the plain along the upper Platte and Wind Rivers.

Angus and his Pawnee were on foot, but

Belzey owned six fat ponies. A fine Crow lodge had been erected by his wives, its skirts lifted for coolness. Robes were spread on its sanded floor. Belzey sat like a king beside the fire on a wolf pelt, eating choice cuts of elk meat which were selected for him by Yellow Blossom, the plump older of the two wives. When his pipe needed refilling, no effort was required on his part. He would merely grunt and Hunts-The-Rainbow, the younger and more comely of his helpmeets, would come hurrying to perform the task.

Zack continued to watch the expressions on their faces as they inspected his raft. The craft carried five packs of furs, bound in rainproofed parfleches. No more than four hundred beaver plews, according to their experience with such things.

He knew what they were thinking. A mighty poor showing for two seasons of trapping and a still sorrier basis for his boast that he would deal with J. K. Fitzhugh's company.

Belzey cleared his throat a couple of times. "Ever hear o' silk hats, Zack?" he asked reluctantly.

"Of course," Zack said.

"Me'n a few other boys got to smashin' every one o' the cussed things we saw last

24

year in St. Louis," Belzey said. "Went thar 'special to do it. Drove them right down over the ears o' the dudes like collars on a plow mule."

"A praiseworthy crusade," Zack declared.

"We got throwed into the calaboose and paid a heap to get shut o' the stinkin' place," Belzey grunted. "But it didn't do any good. Beaver hats are gittin' nowheres, you hear me now?"

Angus nodded. "Plews are down to two dollars, so I understand, and going lower."

"Trappin's finished," Belzey said. "Me, I'm headin' for the Little Buffalo where my squaws' people always winter. Next spring I might take a shuck down to Taos an' raise me a job freightin' to Chihuahua with the lard-eatin' traders."

"Beaver might be finished," Zack said. "But did you ever see a female wearing a silk hat?"

"Ho boy!" Belzey guffawed. "Thet they don't. Leastwise this old he-coon never seed a gal in one o' them contraptions."

"But they're wearing furs for foofaraw and asking for more," Zack said. "At any rate they were two years ago when I took off from St. Louis. Fur coats and muffs and boas.. Fox, mink, muskrat, weasel, cougar, rabbit, and a dozen others."

He drew on his pipe and added, "And there's sea otter. Worth the price of fifty beaver plews. And fur seal. Ever look at a pretty girl in a black sealskin jacket? You just naturally want to bundle right up to her."

"Sea otter and seal come from the Pacific Ocean," Angus said. "Far away. Out of reach."

"And sable," Zack said softly.

"Sable? Ye mean marten."

"Siberian sable," Zack replied.

"Ye talk nonsense, Zachary. Sable is —"

"Ships bring otter and seal pelts to the northwest coast," Zack said. "And sable at times. Rich Spanish *rancheros* buy them in Monterey and San Diego on the California coast, and dress their women in them. Seal and otter. And sable too."

"Sable," Belzey muttered uneasily. "I've heerd of it. Never seen it. They say it's as soft as the devil's voice an' as hard to refuse. Every pelt carryin' with the curse of black pitch."

Zack knew that his companions now suspected that the cargo on his raft was not as unimportant as it had seemed.

They were right. Beneath the parfleche was a layer of beaver plews. And beneath these were sable. Imperial sable. Matched

26

skins. Pelts of a rich dark brown, so dark they seemed a fathomless black. Soft as the devil's voice, Belzey had said, and that was true. Softer than the down on a young girl's cheek. A softness that was meant to go with gleaming gems and the smooth ivory flesh of beautiful women. A richness that entranced the eye and brought the imagination into fiery blaze.

These matched skins would bring perhaps twenty thousand dollars, if marketed wisely. Twenty thousand dollars as a stake with which to go upriver again with keelboats loaded with trade and hard-minded men to pole them, men who would fight and would not fear Fitzhugh Fur.

"Smuggled furs!" Angus Macleod said accusingly.

"Who's to say who is entitled to collect duty on the skins of animals that swim the ocean or walk the wilds of the land?" Zack demanded.

"A lawless concept."

"There's no law on the coast where I stood a few months ago," Zack said. "The Spaniards claim it but never go there, the Russians have a fort on it but don't venture inland, the British are on its edge with trading posts, but no nation really holds it. American trappers know the country

27

better than any of these. A war will likely be fought over it some day, but right now it's no man's country. The furs that are taken or brought there belong to the man who has them and is strong enough to keep them."

"Are you saying you seized furs by force?" Angus demanded.

"I paid a fair price," Zack said. "Mirrors and beads and hawk's bells. And good steel knives. Powder and lead and guns."

"Where would Indians get Siberian sable?" Angus demanded.

"From wrecked ships at times. From Russian pirates who needed food and water and women. From traders. From poachers and smugglers. Even from honest men occasionally. Who knows?"

"Tainted with the devil's curse," Angus growled. "A fair price ye say? Beads. Hawk's bells. Bah! Worthless foofaraw. Ye exploited ignorant savages."

"This foofaraw gave them joy, brought glory into barren lives," Zack said. "The knives, the guns, the powder and lead helped hold back the famine that is their ceaseless enemy. What is a fur coat worth to a kept woman in an eastern mansion? No more than a string of glass beads are worth to a Chinook squaw parading to catch a husband on an Oregon beach. I packed this foofaraw twenty-five hundred miles from St. Louis two seasons ago. I wintered with it in the Shoshone country and nearly starved. Took a Blackfoot arrow in my leg and lay for days in a cave where a bear had hibernated."

He looked at Angus and added, "Do you still believe it was worthless finery?"

Angus wagged his head. " 'Tis a new viewpoint, I must admit." He pointed to the raft. "Ye mentioned the way these pelts were acquired. By bartering the necessities as well as the vain requirements of life. Ye said women may have been sold. I fear ye have sold something too. Your soul, lad. What do ye intend to do with the money ye receive?"

"Bring Logan Brothers back in operation. Pay off the men who had faith in the Logans and loaned us money that we lost when Fitzhugh Fur destroyed us and murdered Dan."

He added, "And some day to get my hands on the throat of J. K. Fitzhugh."

"J. K. Fitzhugh may be old enough to be your grandfather," Angus argued. "At any rate he is far away. He lives in New York, where Fitzhugh Fur was founded a hundred years ago or more by the first J. K.

Fitzhugh. The head offices are still there. J. K. Fitzhugh never comes to the mountains personally."

"I may go to him," Zack said.

"It happened that I journeyed east a year ago last spring on sabbatical leave to report to the board of missions in New York City," Angus said. "I visited the offices of Fitzhugh Fur. They are located not far from the Hudson River docks."

"You know Fitzhugh, then?" Zack asked, his interest flashing like powder beneath the spark. "What is he like?"

Angus shook his head. "It was a busy place with many clerks. But I did not see J. K. Fitzhugh."

"Why not?"

"They told me he was away, sojourning in France."

"A picture?" Zack questioned. "Surely there must have been a portrait of him? He must be vain enough for that."

Angus frowned, thinking. "Now that ye mention it," he said. "It seems strange there was none. Oil paintings of the founder, yes. The original J. K. Fitzhugh, dead these many years. And of J. K. Fitzhugh, the second, and of J. K. Fitzhugh the third, both of whom are also deceased. But none of the present *patron*. It is odd."

"His family? There must be relatives."

"Perhaps. I did not inquire. It didn't seem important at the time. It happens that a very dear friend of mine is the real, active head of the company. Paul Chalfant."

"I've heard of him," Zack said. "The general manager."

"Paul and myself were shipmates when we sailed for America as raw immigrants more than forty years ago," Angus explained. "He is French. I sailed from Bordeaux on a French vessel for the sake of cheaper passage and favorable winds. We became warm friends and have been so ever since."

Belzey Williams spoke, a growl of rage in his voice. "Chalfant! A man to spit on. Now thet you mention it, parson, I recollect thet Chalfant's name was read along with thet o' Fitzhugh on the order which gave me ten an' one at the post."

Angus's frown deepened. "If so, 'twas done without Paul Chalfant's knowledge. I'm certain of that. He might fight ye with bare hands, or pistols, yes, but he is not one to order a human to be whipped, no matter how much ye may have deserved it, ye old sinner."

The expressions on the faces of Zack

31

and Belzey goaded him into further defense of Chalfant. "I know Paul far too well to believe anything else. I have kept in touch with him through the years. Why, it was myself who helped him find a position with Fitzhugh Fur years ago as a clerk in their office in New York. He was steadily promoted until he became business head nearly twenty years ago."

Zack drank coffee from a metal cup and sat thinking. "I've talked to many traders and mountain men, some of whom had been as far east as New York," he said. "They all talk like they know Fitzhugh personally. Yet, when I pin them down, I find that none of them, like yourself, has ever seen him in the flesh. Chalfant, yes. But not J. K. Fitzhugh."

He looked at the river. The sun had gone down and the shadows of twilight were turning to a deep lilac hue. "I'm beginning to think the man does not exist," he said.

Angus smiled. "A ghost? More nonsense."

"One thing's for certain," Zack said. "Quinn Spain's no ghost. He's still the *bourgeois* at Fort Jeanne."

He got to his feet. "Where are you bound, Reverend?"

"Fort Jeanne," Angus said. "I could have

made it today, but decided to camp here in your congenial company and also to point out the paths of righteousness to Belzey. I may winter at the fort. I have never visited this region. My work has kept me more toward the Platte country. There will be much to be done at the fort, no doubt. Souls to save and couples to marry."

"And their children to baptize," Zack said. "I fear the most of them will prefer to wait for a Jesuit missionary to come along, Angus. Another year or two won't matter to them."

"These *Boisbrûlés* always rear quite a crop of young ones while they're waitin' for the preachers to show up and read the words," Belzey said.

" 'Tis a blessing they still wish to embrace holy matrimony after viewing its responsibilities," Angus said serenely. He looked at Hunts-The-Rainbow and added, "I would say that ye soon will be enjoying this same good fortune of fatherhood, Belzey."

Belzey expanded. "Yep. Baby's due in about two moons. Around the turn o' the year, I reckon. Purty good fer an old walrus like me, you hear me."

Zack clapped Belzey on the back, a blow that nearly leveled the mountain man. "I hope it's a son," he said. "Forget about Taos and the lard eaters. I'll be back in the spring with men and keelboats, with guns and traps. Maybe with a steamboat."

"Ye are not moving on now — at night?" Angus asked.

Zack nodded. "I've got to make time if I'm to beat the freeze."

"Ye are aware, of course, that Fort Jeanne is less than ten miles downriver?" Angus asked slowly.

Zack shrugged. "That's one reason why I'm traveling this stretch at night. I'm not ready for trouble with Fitzhugh Fur right at this moment. I'll drift by the fort after dark."

"That is not necessary," Angus said. "Paul Chalfant is at Fort Jeanne, in person, so I understand. He arrived last fall and is still there."

Zack turned to Belzey for confirmation. The mountain man nodded. "I've heerd so too. The big he-wolf come into the mountains with Spain, who had gone east to headquarters. Two of a stripe."

"No, no!" Angus protested. "Zachary, ye need not avoid Paul Chalfant, or Fort Jeanne as long as he is there. I cannot vouch for this man, Quinn Spain, but I will pledge my sacred word that ye will get fair

34

treatment from Paul. He is an upstanding, God-fearing man."

"I heerd it another way," Belzey said harshly.

"From whom?"

"Trappers. Mountain men like me. Indians. They all despise your fine, upstandin' friend. Since he's been at the fort the rum has been watered more than ever an' they shortweight the powder an' lead an' beat down the prices o' plews. They say this Chalfant will feed a horse, fer workhorses are hard to come by in these parts, but would let a man starve. What do you say to thet, preacher?"

Angus made a tired gesture. "I've heard such rumors," he admitted. "In fact that is the reason I intend to winter at the fort. They cannot be true. Paul could not have changed that much."

"Maybe it's the company he's kept," Zack said. "He's had years of training by J. K. Fitzhugh himself."

He moved toward his raft. "I'll still pass up Fort Jeanne and Chalfant," he said. "And Quinn Spain in particular."

"Perhaps it is best," Angus conceded. "I have no doubt but that Spain holds no liking for ye. I understand that the two of ye fought with your fists in the street in front of the Rocky Mountain House in St. Louis at the time ye and Daniel were first organizing your venture into fur trading."

"We fought," Zack said briefly.

"Zack beat the tar out o' Spain," Belzey said. "Thet's one reason the feller did his best to smash Logan Brothers Fur."

At that moment MacDuff, the staghound, came to its feet, racing about and issuing a deep warning growl. Movement was evident in the brush.

CHAPTER TWO

The two Indian women darted for hiding in the lodge. Belzey seized up his Hawken rifle. Zack reached for his own rifle on the raft.

A voice was raised in the brush. "No shooting! We're white men!"

Zack, wading knee-deep, strained to push his unwieldy craft off the sandbank and out of slack water toward the current.

He heard the onrush of feet and whirled, lifting the rifle. Nearly a dozen men, wearing the sashes, leather brush caps and red shirts and striped pantaloons of Fitzhugh Fur *voyageurs,* were swarming into view. Among them were two Mandan Indians.

Their leader was a lean, authoritative, smoothly tanned man with brown, crisp hair and a small, clipped brown mustache. He was a six-footer and in his mid-forties. His skin was tightly fitted over a sharply-cut jawline and a thin, slightly arched nose. He wore Fitzhugh Fur garb also, but his garments were of better cut and texture, and his blue sash was of silk. This was a man of success, who was sure of himself and his future.

Zack held the rifle at the ready. Its muzzle was pointed at Quinn Spain's middle. With deliberation, Spain drew a pistol from his sash, cocked it, and held it carelessly in his hand, its bore bearing on Zack.

They stood thus for a moment, each knowing that if either fired both guns would be touched off and both bullets would find their mark at that close range.

Angus Macleod stepped between them and pushed Zack's rifle down. "Put away your pistol, sir," he said to Spain. "There is to be no shooting."

Spain lowered the hammer of his weapon and placed it back in his sash. "Of course, Reverend," he said. "We received word this morning from an Indian that you were on your way, and I came out from the fort to escort you."

He indicated Zack and said, "I can't say that I approve the company in which I find you. Where did you drop from, Logan?"

"You can study that over all winter," Zack said. "Maybe this same Indian told you that I was floating down the river. Or does it take a crowd of men to escort a preacher?"

He turned to his raft and once more essayed to push it toward the run of the cur-

38

rent. At a nod from Spain, several of his men grasped the craft and held it near shore.

Zack turned and drove a fist against the jaw of a bear-shouldered man with coarse black greasy hair and a flat nose. This was the Boisbrûlé, Jules Lebow, who was always on hand to carry out Quinn Spain's orders.

The blow rocked Lebow, but the jaw was as massive as his frame. He moved back a pace, rising lightly in a grasshopper leap, a moccasined foot striking out in a blow aimed at the pit of Zack's stomach. *Le savate*, the *voyageurs* called this form of combative effort.

Zack was well acquainted with *le savate*. He had anticipated it. He caught Jules's ankle in mid-air, lifted twisting, and hurled the man's bulk in a somersault end over end — almost as he had the log in the caber toss.

The raft was in the way. Lebow's head thudded on a cottonwood length. His skull was hard, but the cottonwood was harder. He slumped into the shallow water, stunned. A comrade dragged his floating bulk ashore.

Zack paid the penalty. He was swarmed under by the others. One leaped on his back, seeking to pin down his arms. Others flailed at him with fists and feet. They were so eager to damage him that they were impeded by their own numbers and their own ferocity. Zack fought back, dealing out bruises.

Angus Macleod came shouldering into the melee, yanking men back, sending them spinning away. "Enough of this!" he roared.

He tore the opponent from Zack's back and tossed him bodily into the water. He stood between Zack and the panting, drenched *voyageurs*.

Quinn Spain motioned his men to stay clear. They subsided, but two of them still clung to the raft, balking Zack in his intention of leaping aboard and departing.

Zack moved toward these two, fists knotted for further battle. "Get away from —" he began.

Angus caught his arm. "Peace!" he said. "Call off your men, Spain."

"Logan asked for trouble, Reverend," Spain said. "We only want to question him and take a look at his plews."

"Why?" Zack demanded.

Spain continued to address the missionary. "We've been plagued by cache and trap thieves. We examine the packs of all unidentified men passing down the river."

"It's a little late in season for trap robbing," Zack said caustically. "Any plews worth the effort were shipped out of your territory months ago. A new season's about here."

Spain glanced at the raft. "Those packs contain plews, from all appearances."

"Taken a long distance from here," Zack said.

"Or kept hidden until you thought it safe to smuggle them out."

"How could you say where they were taken?" Zack demanded.

"Our trappers mark their pelts with the indelible stamp of the company," Spain said. "That's a move we were forced to make because of cache robbing. We have no further interest in you if the mark is not on your plews."

"It'll be there, once you get your hands on 'em," Zack said. "I don't intend to give you the chance."

"You have no choice," Spain said.

Zack lifted the rifle. "No?"

"What good would that do against ten of us?"

"Nine — after I pull the trigger," Zack said. "You won't count."

Spain had rigid control of his emotions, a quality that is called courage. "You have a point," he conceded.

Angus spoke hastily. "End that sort of talk, the both of ye. Ye are being high-handed, Mr. Spain. This should be settled at the fort in the presence of Paul Chalfant. After all, he's your superior. Zachary, I'm sure ye will get fair treatment at Paul's hands."

"Of course," Spain said. "You are an old and dear friend of the grand *patron*, aren't you, Reverend? Paul has mentioned you often and has been hoping all summer that he would meet you again."

"Chalfant's no friend of mine," Zack said.

"Come, Zachary." Angus spoke placatingly. "Surely, ye must admit there could be justice in Spain's position. All they ask is to inspect your pelts. I'll see to it that they are returned to ye."

"My packs are not going to be opened until I open them myself in St. Louis," Zack stated.

He swung the rifle toward the two men who clung to his raft. They saw the gray look in his eyes and sucked in their breaths sharply, each expecting a bullet.

Spain snatched out his pistol and would have shot Zack in the back except that Angus intervened again. He moved in to protect Zack, risking taking Spain's bullet himself. He seized Zack's rifle, jamming the lock with his thumb.

"It is the best way for your sake, Zachary," he pleaded. "I pledge my honor that ye will find Paul Chalfant honest. Put down your weapon again, Quinn Spain."

At a nod from Spain, his men moved in. It was useless to resist. Zack surrendered the rifle to Angus. The *voyageurs* roughly tore the knife from his belt and removed the powder horn and pouch.

Angus stood by, disapproving of relieving Zack of his weapons but unable now to protest it.

"We'll take him to the fort, as you wished, Reverend," Spain said.

"You mean tonight?" Angus asked.

"It's only a little more than two hours by trail," Spain said. "It will be more comfortable than camping here."

"I shall go with you," Angus said.

Zack found that Belzey was gazing at him, awaiting advice. Zack shook his head. Outnumbered, there was nothing Belzey could do except to risk another beating at the whipping post. "See to it that you live to know your son," Zack said. "I'll be back in the spring with a present for him."

Spain ordered Jules Lebow, who was

now on his feet, to float Zack's raft to the fort. Zack, unbound, but a prisoner nevertheless, set out on foot, surrounded by Spain's men. He was accompanied by Angus and his Pawnee who carried their camp gear on their backs. They followed a much-used trail that skirted the course of the river.

Spain had made the journey from the fort mounted on an Indian pony. He offered the mount to Angus.

Angus refused. "These two feet have carried me many hundreds of miles, and I have never had them fail me," he said. "I trust them far better than four legs."

He laid a hand on the head of his staghound. "What would MacDuff think of me if I showed such weakness?"

Belzey, troubled, stood for a time after the foot party had vanished into the brush. At last he reluctantly gave an order. The two Crow women hesitated, gazing apprehensively at the oncoming dusk.

"Better to travel in the dark than to be shot down here an' scalped," Belzey told them.

His wives burst into activity. Within a short time the lodge was struck. All their effects were lashed on *travois* frames drawn by ponies. Soon the campsite was deserted.

Meanwhile, traveling at a long stride, Zack and his retinue covered the distance to Fort Jeanne swiftly and in silence.

The trading stronghold stood on a bluff out of reach of the floodwaters of the river. They were awaited, for torches burned on the log ramparts, the light flickering on the split log roofs of the big trading post and the living quarters of the clerks and *engagés* within the stockade.

"I forgot to mention," Spain said to Angus Macleod as the party entered the main gate, "that Paul will not be here to greet you, unfortunately. He left this morning to visit a Minitaree chief whose people are camped north of the river. He will be back tomorrow. It had escaped my mind."

Zack said nothing. Angus rubbed his chin dubiously but was forced to accept the situation. "Then," Angus said, "the entire matter must be left untouched until Paul returns."

Zack walked to the open gate and gazed at the river. Its surface was aglitter in the starlight. His raft came in sight, a dark shadow near the shore, and crept to a landing, poled by Lebow.

Zack strode down the path to where floating docks of logs flanked a stone levee.

He waited until Lebow had brought the raft alongside. With his own hands he helped moor it.

Spain and two other *voyageurs,* who Zack was beginning to understand were bodyguards, had followed him. Angus Macleod came hurrying.

"I'll sleep aboard," Zack said.

"As you wish," Spain said. "I'll leave men to keep you company."

"Now that's being hospitable," Zack said. "I don't know how to return the favor."

Zack made no attempt to sleep. He lay tense on his buffalo robe, feeling the alive motion of the raft beneath him, hoping for a chance to cut the moorings and go on his way down the river. But at least one of the men who stood guard on the dock was always alert, and came leaping aboard each time he so much as stirred.

Daybreak arrived, and he could not believe that the night had passed with such speed, so intent had he been on his hope of freedom. Dawn ended that hope.

The fort awakened. Indian women came down to the river for water, bearing wooden casks and pails on their heads. They chattered and bathed in the river and eyed the white man with insolent curiosity.

A young Arapahoe girl who said she had been a slave of the Dakotas and had been bought by a Fitzhugh *partisan* as a servant, brought him a tray of food. The fare was plain enough, but the dishes were of fine English china, and the tray and utensils were of heavy Spanish silver, elaborately carved and carrying the liberty-cap crest of Fitzhugh Fur and the company's monogram.

Fort Jeanne had always been noted for its civilized appointments and luxury. These advantages evidently were extended even to prisoners of importance. For Zack knew that, more than ever, he was a prisoner. He had no illusions in regard to Quinn Spain, and Spain would have none about him. The matter of the death of Zack's brother would remain unsettled between them as long as both of them lived. All that stood between them now was the presence of Angus Macleod.

Zack's razor and hone and strop were still in his possible sack on the raft. He asked the Arapahoe girl if she could furnish him with warm water and soap. She complied at a run. She seemed to pity him. It came to him bleakly that she considered him a person whose life was near its end.

Zack hacked away laboriously at the

47

growth of weeks, with the Indian women crowding close around him in an attempt to get a glimpse of themselves in the small mirror the slave girl had provided.

Their giggling and chatter was that of a flock of geese, and the slave girl finally brought him a willow switch. With this, laying it on bottoms, he kept them at a distance.

He surveyed the result of the shave, running his palm incredulously over his smooth chin and cheeks. He strode up the path to the fort with the Arapahoe girl hurrying at his heels and the squaws following in a straggling line, lugging their casks.

He entered the main gate, whose log portals stood open on their great iron hinges. He halted.

The log-built dwelling that was the residence of the *bourgeois,* or agent, was the center of great excitement.

This structure stood at the rear of the compound, flanked by an ornamental flower garden, dead now of frost, which had a birdbath in its center, along with a fishpond and a silver reflecting sphere.

Nearer at hand loomed the bulky trading building with its overhanging portico beneath which were benches for the idlers, rawhide-slung easy chairs for the trader and more important visitors, and the hard-packed earth for loafing Indians.

Across the enclosure were the structures occupied by the clerks and other employees. Two box elder trees and an oak grew inside the stockade. The oak was in the center of the square, flanked by a small platform that was used for ceremonial affairs.

It was to this oak that Belzey Williams had been tied, and it was from the platform that Quinn Spain had read the decree in the name of J. K. Fitzhugh that he be given ten and one lashes as punishment for dealing with Logan Brothers Fur.

The excitement at the agent's house was spreading. Men and women were hurrying in that direction. Quinn Spain appeared in the door and lifted his arm. He said something that Zack could not hear at that distance.

The arrivals halted and many sank to their knees. An Indian woman began wailing mournfully. She sank down, rocking back and forth, and cast dust over her hair and shoulders.

Zack began running also. A woman sobbed, "It is true. The good one is dead. The Black Coat has been taken to heaven."

Zack raced past the kneeling ones and

gazed at Spain at close range.

Spain answered his unspoken question. "Angus Macleod is dead. It was heart failure. He was found lying in his room only a few minutes ago."

CHAPTER THREE

People of the fort continued to pour from the buildings. Zack mounted the steps to the small porch. Spain barred his way. "There's nothing you can do, Logan."

Zack shouldered past and walked through the house, finding his way to the room where Angus Macleod had been quartered.

The missionary's body lay face down on the floor alongside a small table. He had evidently arisen and dressed just before the fatal stroke.

A chair was overturned near the table. The window was open, admitting the sweetness of the warm autumn morning.

Spain had followed Zack and was standing in the door. "A sad thing," the man said. "The stroke must have come so suddenly Angus could not even call for help. He had eaten a hearty breakfast — too hearty, I fear. I brought the tray with my own hands so that he could eat leisurely here in this room. He overtaxed his strength when he decided to accompany us to the fort last night. I blame myself. I should have insisted that he ride my horse."

Zack bent and turned the body over. Angus's hand still held a fork belonging to the heavy silver service of the company. Death was so recent that the fingers relaxed and the fork rolled onto the floor.

Outside, the wailing of Indian women arose, along with a murmured undertone of prayers. The majority of the fort's staff were of the Catholic faith, but all were joining in mourning a man whose life had been devoted to the welfare of others.

Zack got to his feet. He picked up the fork and placed it on the small table, which was bare. He left the building. Spain walked with him as persistently as a shadow.

The keening of the squaws had aroused the half-wild Indian dogs and they were roaming beyond the stockade walls, adding their shrill howling to the requiem.

Emerging from the gate, Zack came in sight of his raft. Men were busy unloading his packs of furs and carrying them up the path to the fort.

Zack whirled on Spain. The man was smiling. He had been joined by his two brawny bodyguards. Something in Spain's face warned Zack that the man was aware of the wealth in sables that was hidden beneath the rough parfleche lashings. Evidently Jules Lebow had investigated the packs during his lone journey on the raft the previous night.

"Five packs," Zack said thinly. "And I have every pelt counted. I'll want them back, every one, undamaged."

Spain laughed loudly. "I admire your brass, Logan. We always hang fur thieves. You know that."

"So I've been convicted already?" Zack asked.

"We took a look at your plews. Some two hundred and fifty beaver pelts carrying the Fitzhugh stamp seems to be sufficient evidence."

"Beaver?" Zack asked. "Two hundred and fifty?"

He saw just the slightest flicker in the man's eyes. Just enough to confirm his hunch. Spain *did* know about the sables.

"Of course," Spain said.

"What about this Paul Chalfant?" Zack demanded. "Am I to see him? He, at least, is supposed to be honest, according to Angus Macleod."

"You'll be given a hearing when he gets back."

"And then hung?" Zack asked.

"No doubt."

"With J. K. Fitzhugh's permission, I take it," Zack said.

"You knew the risk when you robbed Fitzhugh caches. You knew the penalty."

The group of mourners in front of the residence was increasing, but he and Spain were being left strictly alone where they stood in the open stockade gate. They were so pointedly ignored that Zack surmised that the majority of the *engagés* of the fort wanted no part in whatever action Spain planned to take against him.

"There was a time when fur companies were their own law," Zack said. "But the day is over when you could hang a man without having to answer."

Spain smiled. "St. Louis is hundreds of miles away. By the time word got back there next summer who would be interested in what had happened to a fur thief way up here?"

"When will Chalfant show up?" Zack demanded.

"Perhaps by midday."

Spain nodded to his men. Zack was prodded at the point of rifle muzzles to a dark musty half-dugout in a far corner of the fort. He was pushed inside, and the split-log door was chained and padlocked. The only light came from chinks in the structure. A buffalo robe that had shed most of its hair served as a bed. The jail's principal purpose had been that of sobering up boisterous Indians and trappers.

Zack moved to one of the slits of light in the door and peered. The mourning was still going on but the howling of the dogs had ended.

He had been trying to maintain a confident front, but within him was a growing panic. He had depended on Angus Macleod and on the missionary's faith in Paul Chalfant. That ground had been cut away from under him.

"Walked into it with my eyes open," he groaned.

A whiskered, thin-necked guard moved into his line of vision, a rifle slung on an arm. "Did you speak, *m'sieu?*"

"A passing thought," Zack said.

Time crawled by. An hour. Two, according to the slant of the sun. A commotion in the compound aroused him, and he moved to the eyehole. Whatever the attraction, its source was evidently at the docks. An exodus was taking place in that direction.

Zack's guard was talkative. It seemed that a keelboat was arriving from St. Louis. The last of the season. It brought supplies that were much needed for the winter.

The keelboat men presently entered the stockade, shouting and kicking up their heels. The majority were the gaudily clad, mahogany-skinned "half-horse, half-alligator" individuals who had helped pole and cordelle the unwieldy craft hundreds of miles against the current by sheer muscle. They were swigging rum, and some had their arms around Indian girls. They preferred to call themselves *voyageurs*.

Zack's jailer left his post, unable to resist mingling with the throng. The man returned in a dither of excitement.

"Great news, *m'sieu!*" he chattered. "The *voyageurs* bring word that the gran' *patron* is coming in person to Fort Jeanne. None other than M'sieu J. K. Fitzhugh himself."

"Fitzhugh?" Zack exclaimed. "I don't believe it."

"But it is true. Before this boat leave St. Louis word, it came, to prepare another keelboat for a fast journey to Fort Jeanne. The gran' *patron* was to come from New York, where he live, a fortnight after the departure of the ones who have now just safely arrive."

"A fortnight?"

"It will be a smaller keelboat, they say,

and will travel much, much faster. The gran' *patron*, he will be here within a week. Perhaps less. It is a great sadness that the good missionary, the M'sieu Macleod, did not live to share with us the honor of meeting J. K. Fitzhugh."

The man gave Zack a wry smile. "I fear that you will not be here either, my frien'."

"You may be right," Zack said.

Quinn Spain appeared presently, accompanied by two armed *Boisbrûlés*. The door was unlocked and opened. "Come, Logan," Spain commanded. "Paul Chalfant is back. He has a few moments to hear your story."

Zack was marched to the trading post and to an inner room. The *Boisbrûlés* remained outside. Spain, a pistol drawn, came in with Zack and closed the door to shut out the gaze of the inquisitive clerks in the trading room.

One other man was in the room. He sat at a desk, his back to the light from a single window. "I'm Paul Chalfant," he said.

He was a thin, graying person of perhaps fifty, with a sparse, short pointed beard. Like Spain, he wore garments of quality. In this case it was a hunting shirt of doeskin, dyed a cream color and topped with a beaded vest of buffed leather. A wide, brass-studded belt circled his waist, and in it was thrust a dagger and a silver-mounted pistol. It was a swashbuckling costume, but, unlike Spain, its wearer seemed inadequate and colorless.

There was no particular character in the man's features. His nose was thin, his mouth rather small. All in all, it was like seeing a face in a warped mirror and being unable to mark out any outstanding point. Even so, Zack retained a faint impression that he must have seen Chalfant somewhere in the past.

Because of Angus Macleod's glowing praise of Chalfant he had expected something much different. The missionary surely must have been judging his boyhood friend from mistaken memories, or he was a poor interpreter of human nature — an amazing weakness in a man of his calling.

Chalfant was plainly awaiting a cue from Spain. This was given him. "This is the fur thief, Paul. Caught with the evidence."

The man cleared his throat several times. He seemed very ill at ease. He spoke in a scolding voice. "You should have known better than to come into Fitzhugh territory after what happened to you and your kind in the past, fellow."

Zack's brows lifted. "Fitzhugh territory? You mean the Missouri River country? I don't hold that it belongs to Fitzhugh Fur or to anyone else in particular."

Quinn Spain smiled. "Let's stop quibbling."

"What's the charge against me?" Zack asked. "Is it still that the Logans once tried to start a trading company in competition with Fitzhugh Fur?"

"Stealing furs is the charge," Chalfant snapped. "You know that."

"You mean Fitzhugh Fur is spraddling out to claim all territory even to Siberia?" Zack asked ironically.

"What are you talking about?" Spain asked.

"Imperial sable doesn't grow on this continent," Zack said.

"I don't understand your meaning and don't really care," Spain said. "We found beaver in your packs, nearly every pelt carrying our stamp. We've been looking for a thief who robbed caches last winter along the Yellowstone. We've found him."

"You seemed to have only started looking for him yesterday," Zack commented.

Chalfant pounded the desk. "We're going to go easy on you, Logan. You should be hung. However, with Angus Macleod lying dead here at the fort it is a time to be merciful, out of respect to him.

You can thank my old friend that we are being lenient. We will banish you from this country."

"And don't ever come back," Spain said. "There'll be no leniency a second time."

Zack surmised that they were afraid to punish him. It was no doubt true that he owed this in a considerable measure to Angus Macleod, whose presence even in death laid a restraining hand on Spain and Chalfant. But, greater than that, it confirmed Zack's belief that the majority of the Fitzhugh *engagés* at the fort disapproved of Spain and his methods. But, downtrodden, weak-willed, uneducated as they were, they would never openly oppose their *bourgeois*. Even so, Spain evidently had learned to be cautious.

Spain said, "That's all, Logan."

He opened the door and he and his men marched Zack out and through the fort yard to the gate. "All right," Spain said. "Remember! Don't come back."

"Not a rifle to defend myself?" Zack asked. "Or a knife?"

Spain shrugged. He entered the trading post and returned with a rifle, powder horn, and shot pouch. Also a skinning knife. Bystanders watched as he handed them to Zack.

"It's better than a cache thief deserves," Spain said. "But let no man say that Fitzhugh Fur was anything but merciful on Angus Macleod's burial day. It is a tribute to him that we are so lax with you."

Zack hefted the rifle. It was an old smoothbore flintlock that had seen hard use.

He walked through the gate, intending to board his raft. But it was gone. He saw the lengths of the poles floating in the current downstream. The raft had been broken apart. His possible sack lay on the dock. He opened it, but all that it contained was a spare pair of moccasins, and these were worn thin. Everything else had been stolen.

He was being set afoot in tattered buckskins, without even a blanket, hundreds of miles from any settlement. All that he had were the weapons Spain had given him. His tobacco pouch still hung around his neck. It contained only a few scraps of kinnikinnick and his pipe, but it also contained his flint and steel and some shreds of punk impregnated with gunpowder for quick igniting.

The sables that he had packed through the Columbia River wilderness and over the Shining Mountains were in the possession of Quinn Spain.

A young, insolent half-breed came through the fort yard, beating a tattoo on a drum. Zack was being drummed out of Fort Jeanne. Indian and *Boisbrûlé* children gathered and began throwing clods and stones.

Zack walked down the bluff. The children followed him, but when he turned and looked at them, they retreated out of range but kept following him, shouting insults.

Zack entered the river brush below the fort. His tormentors finally gave up the chase. The drumming ended. He followed one of the myriad paths beaten by wood carriers and others in their duties in connection with the fort. Fort Jeanne sank out of sight behind.

He rounded a thicket of brush and halted in stride. Jules Lebow and the two other husky *voyageurs* whom he had marked as Spain's bodyguards blocked his path.

They charged at him without a word. Lebow was laughing, hugely elated by Zack's surprise. The trap was a success. They had been at arm's length before Zack saw them.

He threw up the rifle, but there was no

response when he pulled the trigger. Lebow laughed again and rammed a cocked pistol against his chest.

"I would be happy to send thees ball into your flesh, my frien'," the man said.

Again resistance was useless. Lebow hungrily wanted an excuse to kill him. The man was remembering the fight at the raft when Zack had upended him and rapped his skull on the craft.

The three seized him. A thong was bound around his wrists, and he was marched ahead. They left the path and made their way through the brush for some distance from the river, heading nearer the fort.

They came to a small clearing. Quinn Spain awaited them there. With him was Paul Chalfant. They must have come hurrying from the fort to this meeting place.

Spain held a whip in his hand. It was the long-stocked, single-lash type used by French wagon traders. A wicked implement. It would cut and it could flay.

Zack now knew that all that he had been given at the fort had been a reprieve. They had not dared inflict the punishment in front of witnesses. Spain had arranged it this way.

Zack fought to burst free, but it was useless. Lebow slapped him in the face, slapped him again and again until he was dazed and could struggle only weakly.

They bound him spread-eagled to a tree and Lebow peeled his hunting shirt over his head.

"All right, Paul," Spain said.

The graying man produced a paper and in a shaking, nervous voice read an official order sentencing Zack to twenty and one lashes for the theft of numerous furs belonging to Fitzhugh Fur. The order was declared issued by authority of J. K. Fitzhugh, president.

The whip had the agony of fire, the bite of savage teeth. It bruised the soul and ate at the spirit. It demanded that a man beg for mercy. It insisted that he grovel and whimper. It was wielded at the order of persons who feared the man they were torturing, feared the wrath they might bring upon themselves, but expressing that fear in their own frenzied slashings.

Zack offered none of the weaknesses they wanted to see. He found himself feeding on his own fury which smothered all thought of pain. He strengthened, he towered, as the whip bit into his flesh.

"Harder!" Spain yelled. "Harder! Once more! And again! Jules, swing that thing!"

At last it ended. Jules was sweating. He drew back, uttering a long, indrawn sigh.

Zack waited. Someone severed the bindings. He clung to the tree, for his shocked body would not respond to his will for a time.

When he could think and see clearly again, the clearing was deserted. They had gone.

It was some time before he had the strength to move. He finally made his way to the river and waded in, needing the stinging chill to drive the red curtain of pain from his mind.

He emerged, letting his soaked hunting shirt protect the banded welts on his back. Presently he set out again, heading down-river. They had left him the flintlock and horn and pouch and knife. He tried to load the weapon but found that its rusty muzzle was jammed with a misfired ball that had wedged immovably. The horn contained sand instead of powder. The pouch carried pebbles, not bullets.

The knife was blunted and nicked, and the wooden grip fell from the haft at first pressure. However, the blade seemed to be of good steel and might be sharpened. A makeshift grip could be contrived.

He tossed away the useless rifle. There

was little hope that he might meet friendly trappers this late in season, but his chances of losing his scalp on the plains were excellent.

He debated the thought of hovering in the vicinity of the fort with the intention of waylaying some employee and providing himself with arms, or at least additional clothes with which to face the coming winter.

He surmised, however, that Spain was hoping he would do just that and would warn his men to be on guard. If Zack were caught in such an attempt Spain would have the excuse to have him shot and none of the *engagés* would be likely to raise further objection.

His only hope was to make his way out of the country and to reach St. Louis. Without weapons, he was aware that his chances were slim indeed.

However, there was one possibility. The will-o'-the-wisp, J. K. Fitzhugh, was supposed to be en route to Fort Jeanne by keelboat. The craft should be showing up within a week, according to the talkative jailer.

Aboard it would be J. K. Fitzhugh, as well as weapons. Zack headed downriver, keeping its reaches always within sight.

CHAPTER FOUR

Zack traveled cautiously, day by day, following the course of the river. Wild plums were ripe and these helped sustain him. On the third day he surprised a turtle sunning itself on a log, and its meat gave him a strengthening feast.

He emerged on the fourth day into open plains where the river ran flat and shallow between a maze of sandbars and islands that were festooned with driftwood. It was midafternoon of this day when he caught his first glimpse of other humans.

The white glint of a sail appeared far upriver. He took cover and waited. The craft proved to be a bateau. In all likelihood it had come from Fort Jeanne which was still no more than a hundred miles away. Zack's first thought was that they might be hunting him, but the craft passed by, hugging the far shore. The river was spread so wide at this point that he could not make out much about the occupants of the craft, except that there seemed to be at least three, or possibly four, aboard.

He followed, keeping it in sight, as it

progressed downstream. Although it was still two hours until sundown, the occupants seemed to be seeking a landing place. That turned out to be the case. The sail was lowered and the craft vanished into the contour of the distant north shore. It did not reappear.

These plains along the river were the stamping grounds of the powerful Mandan Indians. Their towns were north of the river. While the Mandans had been friendly to all trappers in the early days, they had become closely allied to Fitzhugh Fur for the past few years and were hostile to all other visitors.

Even though it did not seem possible the crew of the bateau would have any interest in his presence, Zack remained under cover until dusk closed in over the river. If there was any such interest, and if Quinn Spain or Jules Lebow happened to be among the crew of the raft, their intentions would not be friendly.

Zack traveled until well past midnight and was miles below the point where he had last seen the bateau before he camped. He found a gully whose banks were high enough to hide the firelight and flinted a blaze of sagebrush. He was warmed by the embers as he settled down to sleep, but in place of a meal he merely tightened his belt another notch around the leanness of his waist.

It was past midmorning when the faint report of a rifle brought him sitting up, listening. Another shot came. And, after a pause, two more.

The gunfire came from a long distance and seemed to have originated south of the river, the sound carried by the breeze. After a time a grumbling overtone became audible, which grew in volume. A score or more of buffalo appeared over the skyline and passed within easy rifleshot of him. They veered upriver and vanished among sandbanks. They had been running for some time, by the way their tongues were hanging out, and one animal evidently had been wounded.

It might have been Indians who had fired. But Indians hunting meat would hardly have let this herd go without pursuit.

Zack left the river and moved southward, staying to cover in a shallow creek bed. This advantage ended, and he took to the swales. From higher ground he discovered that he was crossing the neck of a great gooseneck bend in the river. He could see the glint of the stream a considerable distance to the east. The distance by water would have been nearly a day's journey, but he came to the river again below in less than an hour.

The stream here was not vacant. A keelboat was being cordelled upstream along the near shore. The long towline extended from its stubby mast to a score of brawny men, bare to the waist, who struggled over rocks and through brush, dragging the sluggish craft against the current, for at this point the water was swift.

Zack crawled to a clump of low brush and bunchgrass almost on the rim of the flood bank and watched the craft creep nearer. The quarters of butchered buffalo lay on the afterdeck. A cook was using ax and saw and knife on the portions.

A hunter in buckskins sat cross-legged on the roof of the cabin, cleaning and reloading several rifles. A bandy-legged, paunchy man in a striped shirt handled the big sweep that served as a helm. He was the *patron*, or captain, of the craft, which was a thirty-footer, modest in size as keelboats go, and evidently not too heavily laden.

A woman appeared from the low door of the cabin. Zack stared, amazed. She was young and very comely. Her hair was a tawny shade and seemed to be thick and well brushed. She wore a calico dress. This commonplace material had been cut and sewn by someone of great skill in the art of enhancing the curve and grace of the feminine figure.

The cordelling crew struggled past, grunting and slithering through treacherous, muddy footing along the base of the cutbank which rose a dozen feet or more at that point. These sounds dwindled as the toiling men fought their way ahead. The keelboat, linked to the human motive power by two hundred yards of towline, crawled abreast of Zack's position. He lifted his head, chancing a glance. The craft was little more than fifty yards away.

The young woman was picking a path past the cook, averting her eyes from the butchered buffalo. She spoke to the captain. That individual glared at the cook. "Cover them things with a canvas, blast your hide, Leon!" he bawled. "Miss Fitzhugh don't cotton to the sight of blood an' such-like."

Miss Fitzhugh? Zack was surprised. It had not occurred to him that J. K. Fitzhugh might be accompanied by women folk.

Another woman appeared. She was in

her late forties, Zack judged, although her golden hair could have belonged to one much younger. Full-figured, she wore a dress with many ruffles in contrast to the younger woman's simpler costume. She produced a snuffbox. With a pink hand she helped herself daintily to a pinch of the contents. She sneezed in a ladylike manner.

The light breeze, with the river as a sounding board, brought their words. The younger one was speaking. "I don't understand why you have taken up that nasty habit, Aunt Sera. You're just showing off. When are you going to stop it?"

"I promise you it won't be while we're in this forsaken wilderness," Aunt Sera sniffed. "Sneezing is my only source of excitement."

A sparrow-thin, gray-templed man joined them. He was neatly garbed in gray waistcoat and tobacco-colored breeches. He wore a cloth top hat, a grave breach of diplomacy in beaver country.

"How about a game of Old Sledge, Seraphine?" he asked.

"Old Sledge?" the golden one echoed. "What's that? It sounds immoral."

"It's a game of cards," the man explained. "The captain taught it to me. It can be played for money."

"Later, Samuel," the woman said. "I'm bored, but not so bored that I have to gamble with a man who'd squeeze a deuce into an ace to win a penny."

"You're being unfair, Seraphine," the man protested. "Just because I keep close account of expenses doesn't mean —"

"Close account? You watch us as though we were embezzlers. Why, I couldn't even buy a pair of stays at that awful St. Louis but what you wanted to know all the intimate details."

"Aunt Sera!" the girl in calico exclaimed. "Lower your voice. We're not alone. Men are listening. Many of them."

"Well, good for them," Aunt Sera said. "It shows they've got ears as well as eyes. I can't even take a bath without a lot of hairy rascals trying to peek."

"It's when they don't try that you'll really start worrying," the younger one said resignedly.

"Too true," Aunt Sera acknowledged. "Did you ever see such a place as this? Flat as the only cake I ever tried to bake. Not even an echo."

She drew a breath, threw back her head and sang a trill. Her soprano voice was powerful and more genuinely golden than the hue of her hair.

She let the sound die away and stood, hand to ear, in a pose of mock listening. "All that comes back," she said, "is the odor of perspiration from our friends on the towline. A familiar companion of our journey, I must say. I hope that you will see that something is done about this, J.K."

J.K.? Zack lifted his head. Obviously that designation had not been meant for the thin, gray man or for the captain. The only other persons in sight were the hunter and the cook. The singing woman's remark could have been addressed only to the young woman in calico.

Zack now saw the name of the keelboat painted on the prow.

Jeanne Kathryn Fitzhugh
St. Louis, Mo.

He kept staring. Jeanne Kathryn Fitzhugh! J. K. Fitzhugh! And there was Fort Jeanne!

It all dovetailed. The present-day J. K. Fitzhugh was a young woman!

He realized that Jeanne Fitzhugh's gaze had turned in his direction. He froze, wondering if she had spotted him, even though he was sure that it would have taken a keen eye indeed to have detected him at that distance which was increasing as the boat crept upstream.

Her eyes moved onward. He avoided any sudden movement, lowering his head very slowly and flattening out in his hiding place. No outcry of discovery came.

"This ark is barely moving, Captain Biggle," Aunt Sera was saying.

"Doin' putty well, ma'am. You ain't used to keelboats yet. Once we round yonder bend we might be able to set sail an' make better time."

"How thrilling. Jeanne, dear, whatever impelled me to let you browbeat me into chaperoning you on this journey I'll never know."

The boat moved out of range, the wind ripples slapping against the hull like mechanical applause.

Zack retreated, crab-fashion, to safer cover. Afterwards, from higher ground, he watched the keelboat work its way upstream. It reached better water, and the cordelling ended. The crew went aboard and began wielding poles. Zack lay there for two hours, watching it recede to toy size, and then to a dot.

By midafternoon it reached the curve of the gooseneck and crawled out of sight below the banks. Presently, a yellow-white speck showed above the plains to the north. The keelboat had conquered the bend and was heading westward again with sail raised to take advantage of a following wind.

Zack had eaten the last of the wild plums the previous day. He had taken in his belt another notch that morning and had noticed that his hands were growing thin, the knuckles more prominent.

He craved meat. All his thoughts while awake and all his dreams were occupied with visions of food. His mind kept dwelling on memories of savory meals and feasts of the past. Time after time, deer and elk and smaller game had appeared, gazing at him as the raft floated down the river. It was as though they had known they were in no danger.

He had seen buffalo near the river the previous morning and had tried to stampede them into a coulee, but they had evaded that trap which might have furnished him with meat from an animal killed in a pile up, or from one he might have been able to dispatch with his knife. They had rushed past him and onward into the plains.

He kept the sail in sight as he made his

way back across the neck of the bend to the upper stretch of the river. The keelboat hove into view some three miles down the Missouri. The wind had shifted, and the sail had been furled. Poles and oars were being used, but progress apparently was slow.

At dusk the craft swung to a landing a mile or more below his position. The crew swarmed ashore to pitch camp. Zack waited until darkness came and moved closer. The glow of the fires began to loom ahead. The contour of the shore forced him at times to wade in the river. He moved with infinite care to avoid any betraying splash.

The bulk of the boat began to take black shape ahead, its mast and combing catching the glint of the shore fires. The evening meal was over evidently, and the party was preparing to turn in for the night. The crew would sleep ashore, the customary procedure except when Indian trouble was feared. Evidently the captain of the *Jeanne Kathryn Fitzhugh* did not fear danger from that source, for there seemed to be no scouts or pickets on duty.

Candlelight wavered in the window of the deckhouse. That vanished as curtains were drawn.

Zack crouched on the shore. The camp had settled down. The glow of the fire faded to a somber hue. He judged that half an hour had passed and he could force himself to wait no longer.

He waded into the river. He was shivering, his teeth tight-clenched. Only that morning, clouds had shut out the sun for a time, and the wind had blown chill and damp. The weather had cleared, and the day had turned warmer. But it had not been the summery balm of the past two weeks. Zack was aware of the dread of winter.

He let himself float, only his head above the shallow water, into the shadow of the keelboat's hull. He hung there, palms pressed against the water-slimed planks.

A gangplank overhead bridged the gap between the craft and shore. But he had been wrong about the camp being asleep. Someone moved from shore across the gangplank and aboard the boat. He saw the sway of skirts against the crimson fire glow. It was the young woman, Jeanne Fitzhugh.

She spoke to someone aboard, but Zack could not make out the words.

It was Captain Biggle's heavy voice that answered. "Now, don't you go worryin'

78

about things like that, Missy. Nobody's goin' to jump an outfit as big as ours. Likely you was only imaginin' things. We're in Mandan country, an' they're mighty friendly with Fitzhugh partisans."

"Perhaps" — and now Jeanne Fitzhugh's voice was more audible. "Let's just say it's a woman's whim. I'm sure I'd feel safer if you put someone on watch."

"All right! All right! If you say so. But it'll sour the men. Tain't easy, standin' guard at night after cordellin' an' polin' a keelboat all day."

"Tell them it's my fault," Jeanne Fitzhugh said. "I'm sure I saw an Indian watching us from the shore this morning."

"It don't mean a thing, even if you *did* see one," Biggle said. "I reckon there's been lots of 'em have watched us, that we haven't seen."

Zack was forced to wait again, and this time in the icy water. Jeanne Fitzhugh had spotted him there below the bend. She had mistaken him for an Indian.

Zack felt the cold seep into his bones as he waited for them to settle down. Biggle went ashore and gave a few orders. After a period of complaining and some profanity and threats, the captain came clumping back aboard, and Zack heard him mutter

79

to someone on deck, "Never seen a female yet thet didn't try to run things."

Zack felt the hunger that was a craving within. He felt all the loneliness and futility of his predicament. A savagery entered him, a desire to smash and hurt and crush.

There had been authority in Jeanne Fitzhugh's voice when she had overruled Biggle. Keelboat *patrons* usually permitted no interference. Biggle had resented her advice but had not dared make an issue of it. Jeanne Fitzhugh's manner indicated that she was in the habit of having her own way.

"A spoiled, rich brat," Zack reflected, his body quivering with the cold.

But there was no longer any doubt now that she was the J. K. Fitzhugh he held responsible for many things. She was the grand *patron* of the company, the employer of men like Quinn Spain and Paul Chalfant.

No sound had come from above for a long time. Zack could endure the chill of the river no longer at any rate. He inched ashore, forcing himself to emerge slowly, letting his buckskins drip silently. He kneaded his numbed legs until they became more answerable to his will.

He crawled to the gangplank. He had a

view of the shore camp. The two fires had burned to a faint glow. If there was anyone awake and on guard he was not visible.

Zack crept aboard the keelboat and crouched below the catwalk. He was amidships with the square bulk of the cabin rising only an arm's length away. The curtained window was dark.

The foredeck, which was partly within his line of vision, seemed vacant. A bollard cut off his view sternward.

He could hear the breathing of sleepers on the aft deck. He crept in that direction and gained a viewpoint. Three men lay there on beds of robes and blankets. The captain and his mate, no doubt. They had turned over their customary quarters in the cabin to their guests. The third sleeper would be the hunter, who was a privileged member of the party and qualified to enjoy the same comforts as the mate.

It was the hunter's rifle and ammunition that Zack had in mind from the start. There would be other weapons aboard, of course. Scores of them, no doubt, but stored he knew not where. He had hoped that the hunter would sleep aboard, rather than bed down ashore with the crew, and that hope had been fulfilled.

He moved toward the sleepers. He drew

the knife from his belt. He had sharpened the blade and had contrived a passable grip. He hoped that, in case it was needed at all, its threat would be sufficient.

He identified the hunter who lay beneath a blanket. The man's rifle stood nearby, leaning against the cabin. The belt, carrying powder horn and pouch, hung from a peg.

Zack managed to appropriate the belt in silence. He reached for the rifle.

Behind him, Jeanne Fitzhugh spoke, her voice shrill with excitement and fright. "Don't touch it. Stand up straight and don't you dare move. There are two of us and we've got fowling pieces aimed at you."

The voice of Samuel Hunter joined in. "We can't miss."

Sam Hunter wore a nightshirt. The girl was still fully dressed, with a knitted cape wrapped around her shoulders for warmth. They had emerged from the cabin door. Evidently they had heard him come aboard and had been crouching there in wait. They had shotguns in their hands.

Captain Biggle, the mate and the hunter awakened, came out of their blankets and leaped on Zack, pinning his arms.

"I told you I saw an Indian this morning," Jeanne Fitzhugh chattered triumphantly. "And I saw him later on through the spyglass, watching the boat from far off. If I hadn't stayed awake he'd have scalped all of us."

She came closer, peering at Zack. "He *is* an Indian, isn't he?" she asked uncertainly.

"Not this here cuss," said the hunter. "He's white, he is. Leastwise he ought to be after he gets some of the mud washed off him."

CHAPTER FIVE

Lighted candles were brought. A ring of eyes surrounded Zack. The golden-topped Aunt Sera joined the group, wrapped in a heavy cloak.

"He looks starved," Jeanne Fitzhugh commented. "What's your name? You're hungry, aren't you?"

Zack decided to pose as an unlettered mountain man.

"Hungry as a flea on a marble dog," he said.

"Who are you?" she repeated. "What's your name?"

"Jack Smith," Zack said.

"How long did it take you to think up that name?" she asked. "What are you?"

"Free trapper," Zack said.

Captain Biggle, who because of his girth was known as Doughbelly, uttered a snort. "Free trapper, huh. So that's it!"

"That's it," Zack said.

"What do you mean, 'that's it'?" Jeanne Fitzhugh demanded.

Biggle gazed astonished as though wondering if she was pretending.

Zack spoke. "Seems like the *patron* thinks you know that free trappers ain't what you'd call welcome in territory that Fitzhugh Fur tries to claim as its own. I think the same."

The girl frowned. "Do you mean you've had trouble with Fitzhugh Fur?"

Zack laughed ironically. "Trouble? You might call bein' given twenty an' one trouble."

"Twenty and one? I don't understand."

Samuel Hunter supplied the information, his voice uneasy. "That is a way of saying that he was given twenty-one lashes with a whip."

Jeanne Fitzhugh drew back a step. "With a whip? Who — who?"

"It was done in your name," Zack said.

"My name? That's impossible!"

"You're J. K. Fitzhugh, ain't you?" he demanded, wanting to make sure of this.

She ceased her instinctive retreat and straightened. "I am. What did you do to deserve this punishment?"

"Ask Quinn Spain and Paul Chalfant," Zack snapped.

Biggle pushed him roughly back. "Now, don't go givin' Miss Fitzhugh none o' your impudence. If you got the cat, you must be a fur thief. From the looks, they ought to have hung you."

"When did this whipping take place?" the girl demanded.

"Five days ago," Zack said. "Five years. Five centuries. What is the difference?"

She understood. The memory would never be dulled by time.

"What'll we do with him, miss?" Biggle asked. "Hang him?"

"Hang him? For what?"

"He sneaked aboard to murder us, didn't he?" Biggle asked virtuously. "He had a knife. An' there ain't no doubt but what he's a trap robber, if they laid the lash on him."

"I wanted a rifle," Zack said. "That was all."

"What happened to you?" she asked, her gaze traveling over his gaunt frame and ragged buckskins. "Why aren't you armed? Was it Indians?"

Zack gave her a thin smile. "Worse'n that, miss."

"Do you want to tell us who you really are and why you were whipped?"

"Now that'd take a heap of tellin'," Zack said.

"You're evidently nothing but a slippery scoundrel," she decided. She turned to Biggle. "We'll take him to Fort Jeanne.

Uncle Paul and Mr. Spain will know more about him than he wants to tell."

Uncle Paul! So Chalfant was kin to her. Zack wondered if there was also such a tie with Quinn Spain.

"How about keelhaulin' him, Miss Jeanne?" Biggle asked hopefully.

"Feed him," she said. "He may be more of a mind to tell us the truth tomorrow."

"If he eats he works for it," Biggle declared. "I can use another man on the rope. There's plenty of fast water ahead an' a lot of cordellin' to do. He looks like he'd make a good one on the line with a couple of meals under his belt. Big as a grizzly. Strong."

"As you wish," she said indifferently, turning away. "But no keelhauling, at least not at present."

The hunter, assisted by the mate who was a towheaded stalwart addressed as Cotton, marched Zack to the foredeck and shackled him to a ringbolt with a length of log chain linked around his waist and secured by a padlock. He had only a few feet of leeway.

Biggle shouted orders, and the cook brought cold meat and bannocks. Zack made quick work of these items, and Biggle called for more.

"You ain't had a solid meal in quite a spell, have you, man?" Biggle marveled. "Wal, eat hearty. We got plenty of meat. You'll need it tomorrow on the cordelle."

The hunter, whose name was Hank Gratt, brought his blanket and robe forward and stretched out to sleep on guard on the deck beyond Zack's reach. Zack, with the unwieldy chain around his waist, found himself facing the prospect of spending the night on the bare deck in wet buckskins.

However, Samuel Hunter brought dry, new garments from the store chest, including a warm mackinaw shirt and striped *voyageur* breeches, items which Biggle vowed Zack would pay for sooner or later. Hunter also supplied a buffalo robe and a woolen blanket.

Seraphine Fitzhugh joined them. "My niece sent the clothes and bedding," she told Zack. "I doubt if you deserve such luxury or are accustomed to it. You look like a perfect rascal to me."

"Nobody's perfect, ma'am," Zack said.

Samuel Hunter spoke. "In case you do not already know, this lady is Miss Seraphine Fitzhugh. She is Miss Jeanne's aunt."

"So I gathered," Zack said.

"I'm Samuel Hunter from the Fitzhugh Fur office in New York," the man explained.

"I came along to look after my niece," Seraphine Fitzhugh said. "Sam thinks he is looking after me."

"You sing real nice," Zack said. "I heard you this mornin', lady. Your voice, it shines, I tell you now."

"Thank you," Sera Fitzhugh said dryly. "That is praise from an unexpected quarter, I must say. I once had high hopes of grand opera. I spent a young fortune on voice instruction on the continent. I now waste the results on prairie dogs and scamps such as you who lurk in the grass. Now just who are you?"

"I told you."

"Yes. You're one of the many Jack Smiths of the earth. I no more believe that than I believe you're as beaten down and ignorant as you pretend."

"Aren't you a far piece from this place where you practiced for the opera?" Zack said.

She studied him. "That is an obtuse way of asking me the same question I asked you. In other words, exactly what am I doing here in this forsaken land? And my niece also? Strange as it seems, I have a feeling that in fairness to Jeanne even a ruffian such as you is entitled to an explanation."

"I'm listenin'," Zack said.

"If you were really punished as you say you were by order of J. K. Fitzhugh, then the responsibility is mine, not Jeanne's," the golden-haired woman stated.

"And if she really is J. K. Fitzhugh, then why's she been hidin' out for so long?" Zack countered.

"She hasn't been hiding, confound you. Jeanne is the fourth J. K. Fitzhugh to head the company. She inherited it when she was four years old. Her father was my brother. Both he and her mother, who was a Chalfant, were drowned in a ship sinking during a storm off the coast of France. My brother, who was John K. Fitzhugh, the third, had been in poor health for years, and had spent the greater part of his time abroad seeking treatments. Jeanne was born in France. I was named her guardian. Samuel, here, has been my guardian by his own appointment."

"You mentioned the name of Chalfant," Zack said.

"Paul Chalfant is general manager of Fitzhugh Fur and has been its real head for years. He was the brother of Jeanne's mother. The three of us, Paul, Sam and myself, did not think it good policy to let it be known in the mountains that the grand *patron* of Fitzhugh Fur was a female. Therefore we maintained the illusion of the mysterious J. K. Fitzhugh as overlord. Jeanne has only recently decided that it was high time she let everyone know the truth. But, until she came of age, I was the one who signed all official papers in her name. I am the one to blame, if you have any honest complaints, not she."

Zack was wondering why this sophisticated but frank-spoken woman was telling him all this. Sera Fitzhugh must have seen that thought in his face. "I don't know why I'm unburdening my soul to you," she said, "except that I have an odd belief that I should do so. I suppose, now that I've done so, I'll never know a carefree moment. You'll likely cut my throat in my bed as a reward."

"You're safe enough," Zack said. "I don't even use a whip on females. No matter how much they deserve it."

"You probably deserved what you got," she said. "You have the arrogance of a lawless person, and the disposition. You are quite sizable. It must have taken several men to subdue you."

"I ain't subdued yet," Zack said.

Sera Fitzhugh peered closely at him in the faint light and sighed. She gathered her bulky skirts and said, "Come Samuel. This man frightens me. His eyes are dreadful."

They went away. Afterwards Zack heard sounds in the cabin which indicated that the two feminine passengers were finally turning in for the night. He stretched out on the robe they had given him and drew the blanket around him. He fought off weariness until he was sure Hank Gratt was sound asleep. He tested the chain, seeking to slip out of the loop. But Cotton had made sure it was tight enough. He finally gave up and fell into exhausted sleep.

A boot, punching against his ribs awakened him at dawn. The sky was shroud gray and Cotton was glaring impatiently down at him. "On yer feet, you. Turn out! Turn out!"

The crew was astir. Breakfast was cooked and wolfed down. Zack was given his share of hot food and he was amazed at how rapidly his vitality returned.

The keelboat was soon under way. It followed slackwater for a few miles. Zack was given a pole and placed among the sinewy keelers whose bodies were hardened to this task.

Working in unison with the others, he took his position on the catwalk. Biggle, at the helm, rumbled: *"A bas les perches."*

Zack and the others set the poles in the river bottom and walked, muscles straining, thus pushing the sluggish craft upstream at the same pace at which they fought their way sternward.

"Levez les perches!" Doughbelly Biggle intoned.

Lifting the poles they raced forward and wheeled, poised for the next thrust.

The process repeated itself, never ceasing, slow mile after slow mile. *"A bas! Levez! A bas! Levez!"* Occasionally Cotton spelled Biggle at the helm and took up the chant. But, for the crew, there was no surcease.

The channel narrowed, and the Missouri's current quickened. Poles and sweeps could make no progress. The cordelle was broken out.

"You there!" Biggle said, pointing to Zack. "On the line. An' if I ketch you shirkin' you'll git another twenty an' one." He turned to Hank Gratt. "Go ashore an' keep an eye on him, Gratt. Put a ball in him if he tries to git away."

For the first time that day Jeanne Fitzhugh and her aunt came on deck as the cordelling crew went ashore. The younger woman ignored Zack, but he was aware that Sera Fitzhugh watched him as the cordelle tightened and the keelboat steadied to this new source of power.

"Ho!" shouted a thick-shouldered keeler next in line to Zack. "Now we weel learn who are the men an' who are the leetle boys. Do not get in my way, young one, or you weel be trampled in the mud like a flattened frog."

"The sail ought to be set again," Zack said. "You have wind enough to drive any boat upriver."

Soon there was no strength or breath either for such exchange. This was work for animals, but no animal would have stood up under it for long. A score of wet, miserable humans, taut hemp cable grinding into their flesh, leaned against the weight of the keelboat, dragging it with them against the current.

Zack, stumbling over brush and slippery rocks, fell full length in the water. The brawny keeler who had taunted him stepped in the middle of his back. He was dragged ahead by sheer momentum as he clung to the cordelle.

He fought his way to his feet, and his tormenter laughed. Jeering amusement ran up and down the line. The keeler, who was known as Big Louie, said, "The mud, eet ees softer than the whip at thees Fort Jeanne, *oui?* You wish to bury yourself in eet like the turtle, no? Big Louie weel help you."

Zack turned, swung a leg, and caught Big Louie below the knees on the same stretch of slippery mud that had been his own downfall. Louie's feet skittered from beneath him and he sprawled in shallow muddy water.

He surged to his feet, enraged, as a roar of delight arose along the cordelle. He came at Zack, arms spread, as though seeking to crush him in bearlike embrace.

This was the classic opening for launching *le savate* as a surprise, a maneuver that Jules Lebow had attempted without success on Zack not long in the past.

Zack stepped inside Louie's arms and drove a right, then a left to the belt. Big Louie's mouth opened in agony. Zack hit him on the jaw with a right, and Big Louie again went down in the shallow water. This time he stayed down. Zack dragged him out of the river and laid him on the shore.

"Proceed," he said to the others. "We have separated one boy from the men."

That ended the hazing. With a roar of approval the line of rough men bent their

shoulders again to the task. Big Louie revived quickly and came scrambling to take
his place again on the line. He bore no
grudge. "You are very queek, my frien',"
he told Zack. "My jaw, eet aches. You hit
very, very hard."

They moved ahead, drawing the keelboat
with them. They stumbled as before over
rocks and brush and floundered in chill
water. Zack again fell at times, as did the
others. But now hands reached down to
help him to his feet, just as he helped
others when they slipped.

CHAPTER SIX

Jeanne Fitzhugh sat on a bench on the fore-deck, a knitting basket beside her, her hands busy. Aunt Sera reclined on a pallet of buffalo robes in the lee of the deckhouse, reading a novel and taking an occasional sip from a glass of wine.

"Faster!" Doughbelly Biggle bellowed from his all-seeing place at the helm. "Faster you lard eaters. An' no more brawlin', you hear me. Save yore strength fer worse water ahead. You, there, Jack Smith! The next time you start trouble you'll feel the bite of a rope end! You're the kind thet has to be beaten."

Zack looked back and said over his shoulder, "Don't force me to add you to my list, Biggle."

The *patron* laughed scornfully. "Sassy, ain't he? A little buffalo brisket an' bannocks in his belly an' he bites the hand that feeds him. He'll be meek before we git to Fort Jeanne, mark my word. I'll see to that."

Jeanne Fitzhugh arose abruptly and went into the cabin, closing the door.

Zack, looking back a short time later, saw that she had appeared again. She had changed from the frock she had been wearing into a dark, heavy skirt and waist and a mackinaw jacket and stout shoes.

The keelboat was almost brushing shore at a point where a clay cutbank arose as high as the deck. Lightly she leaped from the catwalk to land and walked to join Hank Gratt who was ambling along on foot on the crest of the cutbank, his rifle cradled in his arm. Gratt had been maintaining that position all day, keeping watch on Zack, and was bored with his task.

Jeanne Fitzhugh moved along with him. Zack understood. Her pride would no longer permit her to remain at ease on the craft which he was being forced to help drag along up the river against his will.

"Miss Fitzhugh!" Biggle shouted weakly. "Miss Fitzhugh! You'll be safer aboard."

Jeanne Fitzhugh paid no heed. In spite of herself her eyes swung to where Zack was leaning against the cordelle, straining with the others.

"Boo!" he said.

She went crimson with humiliation. She halted in her tracks, glaring at him. "You grinning, insulting, contemptible ruffian!" she blazed. "Captain Biggle was right. You should be keelhauled. Mr. Spain was right too, no doubt. What you need is another touch of the whip."

"Spoken like a true J. K. Fitzhugh," Zack said. "Now I believe it."

She walked on, head high, chin up, ignoring him. Her back was stiff as a ramrod. Her eyes, which were of a shade of dark blue that was almost violet, were very bright with outrage. The keelers were delighted to witness the humiliation of the grand *patron* by one of their number. Grins were passing back and forth, and men were reaching out with boot toes to nudge each other and snicker.

One minced along in exaggerated imitation of the girl's angry stride. She caught him at it. Her fury flared higher, but there was nothing she could do about it without risking further defeat.

But she did not return aboard the keelboat until it had moored for the night. And the next morning, when the voyage was resumed with Zack once more on the cordelle with the others, she again remained ashore, preferring to walk rather than accept an ounce of help from his efforts.

She was willful and also being childish, but as the day wore on and she remained ashore, Zack grudgingly began to concede that she was a person who would not deviate from a principle once she had made up her mind. She would accept no favors from him, no matter the cost.

She was having no easy time of it. Thick brush often blocked the shore so that both she and Hank Gratt were forced to fight their way. Bluffs came down to the river, requiring considerable climbing. At times swampy ground forced her to take to the river's margin, where she waded and stumbled and fought her way through underbrush just as Zack and the cordelling crew were doing.

It occurred to him that she had started to really enjoy this physical contact with the land. She donned a leather brush cap and jacket such as the point men on the cordelle wore in smashing a path through the riverside growth. Wearing this, she often led the way. Hank Gratt, with a true plainsman's philosophy of conserving one's own strength, was very compliant with this arrangement, content to let her bear the brunt of such work.

"My dear Jeanne," her aunt shouted from the keelboat. "You're actually making me ill with all that display of energy. Come aboard and try to sit quiet and ladylike for a moment."

Jeanne Fitzhugh laughed but remained ashore. At midafternoon favorable water and a following breeze ended the cordelling. Everyone came aboard, and sail was set. However, at times the wind faded, and Zack began treading the catwalk with the others, a pole against his shoulder.

Jeanne Fitzhugh had retired to the cabin. She emerged, freshly turned out in a warm jersey dress and knitted cape, with her knitting basket on her arm. Her aunt and Sam Hunter were squabbling over a game of cards in the cabin.

She found a sheltered spot out of the cool wind which was warmed by the pale sun and sat plying the needles while the pole men performed their mechanical evolution to the monotonous beat of Dough-belly Biggle's voice.

Her glance never rested on Zack, but he felt that she was observing him whenever his back was turned. She resented him, resented the way he had entered her existence, jarred her complacency. He had brought doubt to her and uncertainty. He had shaken her belief in herself and in her way of life. The differences between them were vast. She was the sheltered product of good living, and, if her aunt was to be believed, that sheltering had included blinding her to the real truth of Fitzhugh Fur's methods.

In Zack's viewpoint, such blindness was inexcusable. She seemed to know that this was his estimate of her. She wanted to prove that he was wrong and humble him. But somewhere within her was a dread that he might be right. That was where the doubt came in — and the uncertainty.

"*A bas! Levez! A bas! Levez!*"

Zack marched up and down the catwalk, part of a human piston, mindless and supposedly tireless. He watched constantly for a chance to escape, but the chain with which they padlocked him at night and Hank Gratt's vigilance by day had offered no hope thus far.

His body was paying the price of the unaccustomed toil. The cordelling and poling involved unused muscles and sinews. Toughened as he was by the trail and hardship, he found himself keeping step to Biggle's tune only by great effort of will. He longed to drop the pole and to slump down in his tracks to rest.

He kept going, knowing that by so doing he was disappointing Biggle — and also Jeanne Fitzhugh, no doubt.

"*A bas les perches! Levez les perches! A bas! Levez!*"

The westering sunlight dimmed. The beat of the waves against the keel had a dismal, hostile sound. The rippling waters of the river turned a leaden hue.

"Faster!" Biggle shouted. "Faster, you hellions! We're in fer a change of weather. Summer's done fer, you mark my word. Winter's near, an' we don't want to be caught in it."

They camped that night with a cold wind screaming across the plains. Zack sat on shore near a blazing fire among the keelers. He was chained once more — this time to a stout iron stake that had been driven in the shore.

It was a cheerless camp on a sand bar, with only a low riverbank looming behind them to break the wind. Beyond this cutbank stretched the plains.

Progress had been slow. They were still some eighty miles from the fort, with no sign of favorable current or wind to speed the pace.

Jeanne Fitzhugh came ashore as Zack was eating. She had a fur jacket draped over her shoulders. Zack noted that it was of rich, black sealskin. He remembered having said that this was the fur that made every man want to hug the woman who wore it.

She came directly to where he sat. "Un-lock him," she said to Hank Gratt. "I want to talk to him. Alone."

"He might try to make a run fer it, miss," Gratt said dubiously.

"You can stand ready to shoot him," she said. "But at a distance."

Zack, released from the chain, finished his food, taking his time about it, knowing that this nettled her.

"Sorry to keep you waitin', miss," he said. "But I've still got a hearty appetite even for grub furnished by Fitzhugh Fur."

He followed her out of hearing of the others. She was taller than he had first be-lieved. The top of her roached tawny hair came eye-level with him. Her eyes seemed almost black.

"The captain has decided that you are not to work with the crew any longer," she said abruptly.

"Now that's right kind of the *patron*," Zack said. "Was it his idea? Or yours?"

She framed a denial, then decided other-wise. "Mine."

"I'll stay on the cordelle," he said. "I need the exercise. An' the bitter truth is, miss, I'm mighty particular about the kind of company I keep. Now, I'll say good night."

He walked back into the blaze of fire-light. The crew men were sitting, quaffing coffee from tin cups, silent, and studiously avoiding looking either at him or at Jeanne Fitzhugh. They were embarrassed by her presence and also offended by the way she had taken Zack out of earshot. They were likewise avidly curious as to what had been said.

Zack picked up his cup and walked to where the sooty coffeepot hung in its iron frame and poured himself a portion of the steaming liquid. Jeanne Fitzhugh mounted the gangplank and returned aboard the keelboat.

Hank Gratt, the chain and padlock in his hands, arose to shackle Zack. "Here, you. . . ." Gratt began.

An arrow stuck Gratt in the back, the sound harsh and rending. It was so hard-driven from a powerful bow that it pierced entirely through him, the steel head bursting from his chest before Zack's eyes, along with a spurt of heart's blood.

That arrow had been meant for Zack, but Gratt had taken it when he had arisen suddenly. Gratt came falling forward toward Zack, his face twisted in agony. Zack instinctively caught his body and lowered it to the ground. Gratt was dying.

Zack heard another arrow pass close by. The crash of rifles beat over the scene, along with Indian screeching.

Indians in numbers were spilling over the cutbank, shooting and yelling and nocking arrows to strings. Men were dying around the fires. The first volley had wiped out nearly a third of the keelers. The remainder, frozen for a moment, were now scattering in conflicting directions. More of them were falling.

Zack felt the tug of a bullet at his leg. The attackers were pouring into the camp and were now using hatchets and clubs. They were Mandans!

Zack raced for the keelboat, which was the only path of retreat left open. Other survivors were fleeing in that same direction, diving headlong aboard the craft into the protection of the catwalk.

Not all of them made it. A keeler a pace ahead of Zack was hit by the heavy slug from a musket, the ball braining him. He was Big Louie. His body pitched back into the shallow water.

Two others nearby fell short also, clinging wounded to the combing for a moment before dropping into the river.

Zack leaped, grasped the combing, drew himself on the catwalk, and rolled to the deck. He landed bodily on someone crouching there. The person who had cushioned his arrival was Jeanne Fitzhugh. Her eyes were big and dark with fear against the gray pallor of her skin.

The Mandans were rushing toward the boat. One of the crew lay dead on the deck nearby, a rifle alongside him. Zack seized up the weapon.

An Indian reared above the combing, gaining a foothold on the catwalk. He clutched a bow and was snatching an arrow from the quiver that hung on his back.

Zack lifted the rifle and pulled the trigger. The hammer snapped emptily. The gun was empty.

He reversed it, leaping, and swinging it in an arc. The blow broke the Mandan's arm before he could drive the arrow into Zack's body and knocked him from the boat into the river.

Zack swung at another head that appeared over the combing, and the impact snapped the stock from his weapon, leaving him with only the barrel in his hands.

A rifle exploded above him, and another. Doughbelly Biggle was on the cabin roof. Someone was handing him loaded weapons, evidently from a rack where they had been kept handy.

This onslaught tore a hole in the attacking line and gave the defender's a moment's respite. The Mandans wavered.

Zack seized Jeanne Fitzhugh and raced with her to the far side of the deckhouse where she would be sheltered from arrows and flying slugs. He found Sera Fitzhugh and Samuel Hunter there. They were the ones who were passing up the loaded guns to Biggle on the cabin roof.

Sera Fitzhugh also had a shotgun. She stepped past Zack, stood at the corner of the cabin structure, and fired in the direction of the attackers. She ducked back to shelter.

"I don't know how to reload this cursed thing, Sam," she chattered.

Cotton, the mate, an ax in hand, raced to the open prow and severed the forward mooring line. He was killed by arrows before he could reach the stern to free the keelboat entirely.

Zack ran into the open afterdeck, snatched up the ax, and cut the stern line. Bullets and arrows bracketed him, and he could feel the stir of air from them, so close did some of them come, but he reached the shelter of the deckhouse without being seriously hit, although a graze on his arm drew blood.

Four or five other keelers had reached this shelter. None of them had weapons, but there were empty rifles around. These they clubbed and stood ready to stand off the new attack that was being mounted by the Mandans.

Doughbelly Biggle moved to descend to the deck to join them, but an arrow struck him in the throat at the last instant, and he pitched heavily down at Jeanne Fitzhugh's feet and died without speaking.

She had tried to stem the rush of blood with her fingers, but when she saw that the flow had ceased she looked up at Zack and the others, a terrible disbelief in her face. She arose without a word and picked up one of the empty rifles to use as a bludgeon if the need came.

Biggle had carried a knife in a leather sheath. Zack belted it around his own waist. The blade was heavier and of better steel than the one they had taken from him.

The boat was free, drifting along the shore. Zack peered out. The deck was littered with bodies. The Mandans on land were still driving arrows into these limp forms, making sure the keelboat men were dead.

The current was sluggish in the shallows. The boat crushed against overhanging willows and threatened to go aground. But each time it swung free in time.

The Mandans began hurling aboard flaming branches and brands from the cookfires.

"The boat's burning!" Sam Miller said. His voice was calm, as though stating a casual fact.

The port catwalk was on fire. The wind was driving the flames upon the deckhouse.

Zack drew Sera Fitzhugh and Jeanne close. "If we go into the river, stay with me," he told them.

"I can swim," Jeanne said. "I'll be all right. I would thank you if you would look after Aunt Sera."

The deckhouse burst into flame. The heat was scorching. Zack and Sam Hunter protected the two women from this as best they could with their own bodies.

The boat slowly revolved end for end, a deadly maneuver for the besieged because it brought them around into full view of the warriors on shore. Bullets and arrows raked the deck, thinning the ranks of the defenders.

Zack again spoke to the two women.

Sera Fitzhugh apparently was resigned to whatever was to come, and there was no panic in her. Jeanne, however, seemed dazed. He had to shake her slightly until she looked at him.

"We'll have to make a run for it," he said. "Do you understand? The prow is clear of fire. We'll cross it and jump into the water on the outstream side and hang onto the hull. We might drift out of range. Get ready. Don't stop, once you move into the open. They'll be shooting at us."

The keelboat's motion had quickened, for it had been touched by the main current. It was veering away from land. Zack saw that it was already a hundred feet or more from shore.

"Confound it!" Sera Fitzhugh spoke. "How do you work this thing?"

She was trying to load a rifle, but without success. A *voyageur,* an arrow in his stomach, took it from her grasp and handed her a loaded weapon which he was too far gone to steady on a target. "Shoot one for me, mademoiselle," he said.

"I will," Sera Fitzhugh promised. She peered over the catwalk behind which they were crouching and, ignoring the arrows that buzzed around her, aimed the rifle and fired. Zack saw an Indian stagger and

111

fall. It may not have been her bullet, for other weapons were in action on the keel-boat.

She lowered the rifle. "Oh dear!" she moaned, suddenly horrified. "I shot a person."

"Here we go," Zack said. "Hold onto me, both of you."

He looked at Sam Hunter. "Can you swim?"

"Expertly," Hunter declared in his precise tone. "Don't bother about me. I'll be all right. Just see to it that —"

A musket ball struck Sam Hunter in the chest, ripping the breath from him, the impact driving him violently back. He clutched dizzily at the catwalk. His legs buckled and he fell.

Sera cried out and knelt beside him. He looked up at her. "You should have married me years ago, Seraphine," he told her chidingly. "You know that. Now it's too late."

He did not speak again. Sera lifted his hand in both of hers. "Sam!" she moaned in a hopeless voice. "Oh, Sam. And there's nothing I can do now to make up for it."

Zack lifted her to her feet. "Mourn him a lot," he said. "It seems he was worth it. But there's no time for it now."

"He could not swim," she said, as though that explained what kind of a man was Sam Hunter. "He only said that."

Jeanne helped lead the grieving Sera away. The keelboat was beginning to blaze from prow to stern.

Zack seized the arms of the two women and they ran the gauntlet across the open foredeck. They were only in view a few seconds amid the smoke and heat. Zack knew that his hair was singeing. He saw Jeanne's skirt begin to burn.

A volley of slugs and arrows raged around them as they reached the bow and leaped overside into the dark river. They went deep. Zack fought and fought to rise with the two women. Sera was helpless, and while she maintained the presence of mind to offer no resistance or to impede his efforts, she was a heavy burden.

Jeanne Fitzhugh seemed to have weakened. She was moving only feebly in an effort to reach the surface. Zack's lungs were in agony, and this torture drove into his stomach. He would have started swallowing water in the next moment, but was spared that. Their heads emerged.

They floated, gasping, wheezing, on the offshore quarter of the boat, the blazing craft sheltering them from view of the

Mandans. Sera Fitzhugh's head rested on Zack's shoulder, and she was so limp he believed she might even have drowned. But she was alive, for she stirred and began to breathe in a strangling, moaning effort.

Jeanne Fitzhugh was evidently more at home in the water and knew at least the rudiments of staying afloat. She laid a hand only lightly on his shoulder for support, just enough to keep her head above water.

He paddled closer to the boat and found a fingertip hold on some imperfection in the planks of the hull. This gave him a chance to rebuild his own strength.

The keelboat was drifting faster with the current and was continuing its aimless revolving. Again they were brought into view of the shore, but the shadow of the overhang concealed them. The boat was nearly a hundred yards out now, and apparently they were not visible, for while shots were still being fired, few came dangerously close to them.

The blazing craft lighted the shore. Zack glimpsed one figure in a blanket coat and leather cap. White man's garb, although garments like that were treasured by Indians also if they were to be had.

He fancied that he heard a deeper voice

among the howling of the Indians. It seemed to him as though someone was shouting in English, "Find them! Find them!" But that must be imagination.

He worked his way with his companions around the prow to the outriver side so that they were again sheltered from the sight of those on shore. A handful of other members of the crew were around them in the darkness, clinging to this slim thread also.

The keelboat was being carried toward mid-river. Zack became aware of the icy grip of the water and of his own exhaustion. He could hear Sera Fitzhugh still laboring for breath. He drew her closer against him and talked to her. "Hang on! We've got a chance now. We're drifting out of their reach."

Jeanne Fitzhugh was breathing hard also. There was an irregularity in that sound that aroused him.

"Are you hurt?" he asked.

She did not answer. Her hand slid away from his shoulder. Her face, a chalky blur in the smoky glow of the flames, sank beneath the water.

Zack caught her by the hair and drew her back to the surface. Her head sagged. She seemed to have fainted.

"Jeanne!" Sera gasped. "Jeanne!" But there was no answer.

Zack believed that he again heard the deep, authoritative voice on shore, but this time it was using the Mandan tongue, although he felt that it was a white man who was talking. The sound was gone before he could focus his tired thoughts upon it, overridden by the wind and the roar of flames.

An explosion shook the keelboat. Debris and a plume of smoke ballooned upward. The fire had reached the powder supply in the deckhouse.

That reverberation jarred Zack. Before he could make any move a second and far greater detonation came. Evidently the main store of powder in the shallow hold had been touched off.

The hull was torn away from Zack's frail hold. A fountain of flame rose high above them. Along with it went portions of the deck and cabin.

The keelboat was blown apart. Zack saw the black hull which had been their salvation heel ponderously down upon them. He managed to get a tighter grip on the two women as it pushed them beneath the surface. They scraped along the rough planking driven by boiling crosscurrents. A surge of water finally swept them to the surface, gasping, and in the first stages of drowning.

Those seconds beneath the water probably had saved their lives. During that interval the heavier portions of the wreckage that had been blown into the air had plunged back into the river. Smaller fragments were still splashing around them.

Smoke and steam fogged the river. Murky light came from floating debris that still burned weakly. A sizable section of the hull came porpoising sluggishly into view and floated there bottomside up, riding a foot or two above the water.

Kicking with his legs, Zack fought his way with the two women to this floating haven. Sera clung to the hull with her own strength, leaving him free to look after the younger woman.

Jeanne Fitzhugh was unconscious. Perhaps dead. Burning wreckage drifted nearer and in that light Zack saw that blood was flowing from an injury that extended from above her temple into her soaked hair. An arrow or a bullet had grazed her.

He lifted her head higher. His hand touched something. The head injury was not the only wound Jeanne Fitzhugh had sustained during that dash across the prow of the keelboat. An arrow was imbedded in her body just below the right breast.

There was now little doubt in Zack's mind that he held in his arms a person who was so close to death there was little hope. Perhaps she was already gone, and a sorrow came in him. Even though she was J. K. Fitzhugh she was a lovely young woman and this was a weird place in which to disappear, far from the world where she belonged.

But he discovered that she was still breathing and he tried by his own force of will to encourage her to cling to life. "Hang on!" he kept saying. "Hang on!"

Sera Fitzhugh drew closer, gazing into her niece's pale face. "It won't make any difference," she said. "None of us will get out of this alive."

Zack became aware of the same sounds Sera had heard. Paddles were splashing water. The Mandans had manned their canoes in which they had crossed the river and were approaching to search the wreckage for survivors. Others on shore were following the drifting debris. They were building brush fires and lighting torches in an attempt to make sure no prey escaped.

Zack saw that the current was now swinging them back toward the shore where this danger waited. They were a considerable distance downstream now and had drifted clear of the smoke. Only the darkness was in their favor.

The stream's margin at the point toward which the current was carrying them seemed to be thickly grown with brush. At least this would keep the Mandans off the water's edge.

Zack's feet touched bottom. He spoke in Sera's ear in a bare murmur, for a torch glowed on shore just beyond the brush. "Stay in the water. We'll try to hide under the brush."

With Jeanne Fitzhugh in his arms he led the way through the shallowing water, crouching and moving very slowly so as to avoid sound. Torches were shining in canoes on the river, but the Indians had moved on past on shore, depending on their comrades afloat to search the margin of the thicket.

Zack parted the willows which overhung the water. The branches were nearly bare of foliage but flotsam and dead leaves had been trapped by the interlaced growth so that they had a passable screen back of which to lie, bodies buried half in water, half in mud with only their faces above the surface.

Jeanne Fitzhugh stirred and moaned in Zack's grasp. She was returning to consciousness. He spoke to her. "Don't make any sound. We're in the river with Indians around, hunting us. We're hidden beneath brush. Do you understand?"

She did not understand. She was too far gone for that. She began to struggle. "Sera!" she sobbed. "Aunt Sera! Where are you?"

"I'm here, Jeanne, dear," the older woman said.

Reality seemed to come to Jeanne. She murmured, "Jack Smith," and sank back into her stupor.

Presently Zack could hear the splash of paddles coming nearer — fast. He waited, for he felt that they must have heard the girl's outcry. He knew that Sera shared with him that infinite moment of helplessness.

The splashing became louder. A man yelled in horror, the sound so close by it seemed to echo in their hiding place. The outcry came again and was cut off by the grinding sound of a blow, as of a hatchet cleaving a skull. Along with it came the grunting, fast-breathing savage elation of victors.

One of the surviving keelboat men had been overtaken as he attempted to reach shore and slain. That sequence was repeated twice as two more swimming men were located and dispatched.

Zack heard Sera sobbing. "Hang on," he said. "Don't go to pieces now. We're still alive."

The canoes drifted away. Presently the torchlight strengthened. The Mandans were returning upstream, both those afloat and the searchers on shore. Zack heard the Indians talking. Their attitudes were those of men who believed a task was finished.

At best it was the Indian nature to shrink from warfare in darkness, for it was the spirit of the night that was to be feared most of all. The Mandans had given up the search.

The slap of paddles faded off into the distance and silence came. Zack emerged from the brush and, after a time, became convinced that it was over with, for the moment at least. The glow of torches showed upriver. That was where the massacre had started.

Jeanne Fitzhugh was still breathing with labored effort when he returned, but he knew that she could not survive much longer if she remained in the chill water.

He lifted her, and with Sera following, waded downstream along the margin.

The black shape of a bluff loomed up like a gigantic haystack against the night sky a short distance back of the river. It was a massive rock formation, and its base extended to the shore and evidently beneath the stream itself.

Bare rock offered a path of escape from the water which would leave no tracks. "Step only on clear rock," he told Sera. "Avoid any hollows where there might be dust or sand. They'll give this country a real close goin' over tomorrow."

He led the way. Jeanne Fitzhugh was wearing a dark-colored dress, evidently of some warm woolen material, and also evidently with more than one petticoat beneath. The dangling folds of the wide, wet skirts kept entangling his legs, impeding him somewhat.

Sera was equally burdened with layers of soaked garments. Both she and her niece had lost their slippers in the river. Sera was finding the going painful, with only fraying stockings to protect her feet. Zack still had on his brogans that had been given him on the keelboat, but they were filled with sand and small pebbles and water and there was no opportunity to do anything about it.

They followed the rock footing to the base of the bluff. The eminence proved to be a solitary outcrop which rose some two hundred feet above the river and the flats around.

Reaching a niche where a ledge sheltered them from the wind, he placed Jeanne Fitzhugh down. Her scalp injury still bled slowly, but this damage was minor compared to the other.

He explored the arrow wound with his fingers. She wore no stays. The shaft was driven almost through her body. The point lay just beneath the skin near her shoulder blade. Ribs were evidently damaged. It was a harsh, shocking injury, but he doubted if her lung had been involved. Otherwise she would not have remained alive this long.

Sera crouched over her niece, massaging her wrists in an effort to fan the spark of life. "She's dying!" she said. "She's so cold. So cold. What can we do?"

Zack carried the unconscious girl farther around the base of the bluff until they were shielded from view upriver where the flicker of torches was still visible.

He still had his tobacco sack on its thong around his neck, containing the flint and steel and the prepared wick in its watertight case. The knife was still in the sheath at his belt. He found a sheltered spot and placed the girl on a flat slab of rock. Scraping together dry twigs and leaves, he ignited a fire.

"I'll hunt for a better place," he said. "Keep her warm. I won't be far away at any time."

He moved off into the darkness. The south base of the bluff dwindled away into what seemed to be a brushy swamp. He found that it was dry now and firm underfoot. It was thickly grown with brush and littered with driftwood, some of which was mature trees that had stranded here during freshets in the river.

He crouched down suddenly. The snuffling and movement of animals came from ahead. Elk were scattered among the brush, evidently using this as a yard for nightly forage.

He retreated slowly, thankful that he was downwind from the band. Stampeded animals might head upriver and be heard by the Mandans who would suspect the cause.

He retraced his steps and finally mounted the bluff itself. Its flanks were shattered and faulted, making the ascent easy. Though there were many crevices, he could locate none that seemed adequate as a hiding place.

The icy wind against his soaked garb was an enemy of growing strength as much to be reckoned with now as the Mandans. Inaction was a peril. The bluff rose to a rounded knob that reminded him of a buzzard's head because of the way it glinted baldly in the starlight. He paused just short of the last six-foot ascent to this barren summit, for it seemed wasted effort to make that lunge upward.

He started to turn back for further search below when he was startled by a flapping and commotion. A sizable bird rose into the air a few yards from him, apparently emerging from the bare knob. It flew off into the windy darkness. It was an owl, he realized, a great horned owl by its size.

He vaulted to the surface of the knob. At eye-level it had the aspect of an unbroken surface of weather-polished rock. It was larger in area than it had seemed from below, being forty feet or more across.

It was not unmarred. The knob was split almost its length by a fault. Peering, he found that it was floored with dust and debris and was no more than ten feet deep at its most extreme point and was much shallower elsewhere. He descended into it, exploring it mainly by touch of hand. At one point a wall was undercut for a few feet, forming a shallow alcove that would give some protection from weather. The slit narrowed and tapered out at its southern extremity, but elsewhere there was ample depth for hiding three persons, although the quarters would be considerably cramped between the walls. The mat of dust and rubble underfoot seemed dry, indicating that the rock beneath was fractured, letting rain drain off into the strata of the bluff below.

There was no telling but what the crevice might be visible from vantage points below. It might even be known to the Mandans. However, the presence of the owl, whose big nest filled the northern end of the slit, indicated otherwise.

Zack descended the bluff in a rush. He extinguished the fire. Carrying Jeanne, and with Sera struggling at his heels, he ascended to the knob and lowered his burden down into the hiding place.

The walls shielded them from the wind. The owl's nest also was a windfall, for it furnished a supply of dry twigs with which to feed the fire that he flinted.

He descended the bluff once again and returned with more fuel that he gathered from driftwood on the fringe of the dry swamp. He made a mental note to hide all trace of their activity below as soon as daybreak came.

He huddled over the fire a moment, his lungs laboring, holding his numbed hands to the warmth. He believed that Jeanne Fitzhugh was unconscious, but now she spoke faintly.

"Are you still here, Sera?"

"Yes," Sera said. "Oh, yes. I'm so happy you can talk to me, darling. Are you in pain?"

"Is the man, Jack Smith, here also?"

"Yes," Sera replied. "We're hiding among rocks not far from the river."

Zack lifted Jeanne Fitzhugh's hand and sought for the pulse in the wrist. It was there. Its beat was slow, but not as feeble as he had feared it might be.

"The Indians will see the fire," Jeanne said faintly.

Zack pressed a finger on an eyelid, turning it gently back. The pupils of her eyes were dark with suffering, but they followed him questioningly. She still had full control of her muscular reactions.

He added more fuel to the flames so that they leaped high, their heat reflecting from the walls.

"I tell you they will come and kill you," she protested, her voice faint and dry.

"They're a piece upriver," Zack said. "I doubt if a fire can be spotted from where they are. We're on the very topknot of this gout of rock. There's nothing above us for a fire to reflect against."

She tried to pull a knowing smile to her lips. That failed, but she managed a slanting look. "You're not very convincing when you try to delude a person," she whispered. "I know why you're building that fire, Indians or no Indians."

Zack turned to Sera. "That arrow's got to come out. Get her out of some of these clothes."

"You'll have to help me," Sera said. "It will spare her some of the pain."

Together, they stripped the sodden upper garments from Jeanne Fitzhugh. The war arrow was a brutal intrusion upon flesh that was femininely smooth, womanly rounded. She was gorgeously formed.

She lay watching Zack from beneath drooping eyelids. "A scandalous situation," she murmured.

Zack moved out of sight and whetted the knife as best he could on a rock. He returned and spoke to Sera. "Stand by now. First, tear up a petticoat for bandages."

He bent over Jeanne. "Make up your mind that what I do is only for the moment. It will be over with in a hurry. It doesn't count. What counts is living."

She made no sound, but he could see that she was torn by agony. The arrow would surely kill her, if not from actual injury, from torture. It must be removed. But that ordeal might be too much for her. A bleak choice.

He delayed for a moment, afraid and also regretful that such a decision should be in his hands alone. She was still watching him. "You must try to take it out if you have the courage," she said.

"If I have the courage?" Even in this moment she was trying to maintain dominance over him.

Sera spoke. "Jeanne, are you sure you're strong enough to — ?"

Jeanne halted her. "She doesn't understand," she said to Zack. "She doesn't know that I have no choice. You have no choice either. This must be done. I feel sorry for you."

"Close your eyes," Zack said. "This will hurt. Yowl as loud as you want. Screech. That helps."

"You seem to know," she said. "You seem to have done things like this before."

"Three or four times. Once I took a Blackfoot arrow out of my own meat. It hit me in a hard place to get at. I was runnin' like a whitehead for cover when I got punctured. Couldn't set down to my vittles for months. I yelled calfrope so loud as I was takin' it out of my bottom I forgot all about it hurtin'."

As he talked he turned her on her side so that he could see clearly the purple area beneath which lay the head of the arrow.

"Tell me more," she breathed. "Your conversation is entertaining, even though you keep forgetting —"

Zack made two swift slashes with the knife, penetrating to the arrowhead, so that it could be pushed entirely through with a minimum amount of damage. Reaching across her body, he forced the feathered shaft forward, praying that it would not break inside her bosom. It held.

She had begun screaming when the knife penetrated her flesh. She gave one great agonized cry as he moved the arrow.

Blood was spurting. The arrowhead emerged. He broke it from the shaft and withdrew the shaft by the way it had entered. He worked with measured speed. It had all taken but seconds.

Jeanne Fitzhugh saw the satisfaction in his face and knew that the worst of the task was over. She was accorded mercy.

She sank back into a stupor and, for a time at least, did not consciously know pain. Her head rolled back, and her body went limp. Her skin was the pure hue of snow.

Zack looked at Sera and it was as though an icy wind had reached inside him. "I've killed her," he said.

"No," Sera spoke. "She's still on this side."

So faint was the flicker of this life that even the flow of blood was slow, very feeble. They conquered this with the bandages. Zack went to the river and returned, bringing soaked clothes in lieu of any other water-carrying receptacle.

There was little else they could do. Sera again tended the scalp injury as though it were suddenly important. "It will leave a scar," she said. "How unfortunate."

"That was done by a bullet," Zack said. "Someone notched mighty close on her."

"I heard one of our men say that they were Mandans," Sera said. "But I am sure that the Mandans have always been friends of Fitzhugh Fur."

"At least they were Mandans right enough," Zack said.

"How terrible. There must have been some awful mistake. Why would they go on the warpath against anyone, least of all one of our boats?"

"You named it, most likely, ma'am."

"What do you mean?"

"A mistake," Zack said.

"But I don't understand." She was silent for a time, then said slowly, "Or perhaps I do. You mean they thought it was some other party. A boat belonging to another company, perhaps?"

"Such things have been done before," Zack said.

Sera straightened. There was the same hauteur that he had seen in her niece. "Not by Fitzhugh Fur," she said.

"Are you sure?" he countered.

She glared at him, but he saw that she suddenly was not at all sure. In her was the same uncertainty he had seen in her niece when the ethics of Fitzhugh Fur were being discussed.

She shifted to another subject. "Why have you done this?"

"Done what?"

"Stayed with us. Helped us."

It was Zack's turn to glare. "You're women, aren't you? What else could a man do?"

"I didn't notice any other men bothering," she said.

132

"Not even Sam Hunter?"

That hurt. "Of course," she said. "I have not forgotten him. I never will. Don't be cruel please. But the truth is that we attached ourselves to you. And you haven't had the heart to turn your back on us."

"This is useless palaver," Zack said. "I've got no time for it."

"You're not what you pretend," she said. "When are you going to tell us who you really are and why you came aboard the keelboat?"

Zack eyed her. Her dress clung soddenly to her ample figure. Her hair hung in tatters. She was ice-pale as she huddled beside her niece. Her lips were almost blue.

"Get out of the wet clothes," he said abruptly. "Spread them to dry on rocks. Better yet, I'll set up some sticks to hold them near the fire. They'll dry fast. You can lie with your niece close to the blaze. You'll keep warm."

"What about you?" she asked. "You're soaked too."

"Later," he said. "I'm going out to look around."

CHAPTER SEVEN

Zack left the hideout and scouted the surroundings. The night was without sound. It was a peace so intense his pulse gave it the semblance of possessing a throbbing heart. The Missouri was a pale ribbon, curving across the blackness of the plains. Ripples glinted here and there where the current broke over snags.

He scanned the bluff from every angle, seeking to learn if the firelight was visible. Only from one point south of the eminence could he make out a tiny glint, and even that might be mistaken for a star. In any event there seemed little danger from that direction for the time being at least.

He returned to the knob. Its location had the advantage of commanding miles of country and a considerable stretch of the river. He began to believe they had stumbled upon a refuge that might pass undiscovered mainly because it was in plain sight.

He called out softly as he approached the crevice, and Sera responded, "Come in."

He dropped into the cleft. The fire was burning low, and he added fuel. Sera lay huddled with Jeanne Fitzhugh beneath a few of their garments that had dried.

"She's sleeping now," Sera whispered. "The pain is less, I believe."

Jeanne's eyes opened, and she gazed at Zack. "You use the knife well, fur thief," she murmured. She drifted off again.

Zack dried his garb and soaked up heat until he was at last able to sleep. He awakened before daylight. He extinguished the last live embers of the fire, smothering each brand carefully to make sure it would not give forth any betraying odor of smoke.

"We'll have to tough it out for a while," he said. "I think we'll have visitors out there before long who'll be lookin' for signs of anyone who might have crawled out of the river alive."

Sera lay clasping her niece against her for warmth. Both of them wore the torn and wrinkled dresses and petticoats in which they had emerged from the Missouri.

When thin daybreak came, Zack descended the bluff and painstakingly wiped out traces of the first fire he had built and removed what evidence he could find of his wood-gathering activities.

Returning to the Owl's Nest, he settled down to wait. It was two hours after full daylight had come, when, peering from a lookout between broken rock on the rim of the hideout, he glimpsed a Mandan moving along the shore of the river, scanning the ground.

Others appeared. He watched them halt at the rock formation which extended from the base of the bluff into the river. Such a pathway was, of course, naturally suspect.

The bluff became the point of interest for the Mandans. They circled its base, appraising the rocky slants keenly. One lifted a whistle, and more Indians appeared and came hurrying until there were nearly a score in sight.

Under orders of one who wore the feathers of a sub-chief, they began mounting the bluff, peering into every crevice. Zack lowered himself to the floor of the niche.

Sera was awake, staring at him, frightened, knowing from his expression that they were in deadly peril. Jeanne still lay in a stupor. She was breathing fast, moaning occasionally as pain drove through her.

Zack motioned Sera a warning for absolute silence. He moved to the wounded girl and stretched out beside her, his head propped on an elbow. He spoke in her ear. "Can you hear me, J. K. Fitzhugh?"

He was murmuring, but there was an intensity in his voice that reached through the veil of weakness. Her eyes drooped open, regarding him at close range.

"Do you know me?" he asked. "Do you remember where we are?"

Her eyelids fluttered in an affirmative. "I woke you because it's important that none of us make a sound," Zack went on. "The Mandans are out there, climbin' the bluff, huntin' us."

Her dry lips moved. "I'll be quiet."

Her eyes closed exhaustedly. But she was still conscious. Her moaning and heavy breathing stopped. Her courage and her will were stronger than pain and weakness.

There was nothing more that could be done. Zack had the knife. If the Mandans came he would try to use it rather than die passively. But he knew he would be cut down before he could make much use of his inadequate weapon.

Sounds came nearer. The Mandans were talking. A laugh came. Rock clattered down. More laughter and a cackle of jeering talk. Someone had slipped and taken a fall. The others were deriding him.

Zack drew a deeper breath and looked at

Sera, a flare of hope in his eyes. The Mandans had the attitudes of men who believed they were putting themselves to useless trouble. Searchers in that frame of mind might be careless.

He touched Jeanne's hand reassuringly. Her fingers were very cold. They were slender, sensitive fingers.

The jeering and horseplay continued on the bluff. The Mandans evidently believed that if there had been any survivors of the keelboat they were a long distance from this vicinity by this time. They were in a hurry to get this task over with so that they could return to their towns with their loot where they could strut and feast for days and count their coups and boast of their valor in the fight with the crew.

Their voices sounded so nearby that Zack braced himself, the knife in his hand, ready to leap the instant a head appeared above the rim of the crevice.

But no Indian took the trouble to make that last effort upward to the crest of a knob that seemed so barren. In the next instant he heard them descending the bluff, whooping in the disgruntled way of warriors who feel that they have been made to lose face.

Zack saw that Jeanne's eyes were open

again, gazing gravely at him. "Whew!" he murmured. "My topknot felt mighty loose for a minute."

"Have they gone?" she asked.

"Sounds like it. This Owl's Nest doesn't show from below. The only way you can stumble onto it is to climb right on top this bald knob. An' it doesn't look worthwhile. Leastwise to an Indian who's got it in his head that he's wearin' out his moccasins for nothin'."

Zack returned to his observation point. The searchers had left the bluff and were moving on down the river's margin. Debris from the keelboat had drifted ashore at various points and the Mandans were more interested in investigating this for loot than in the laborious task of scanning the earth for tracks they believed did not exist.

Zack was certain there must be other survivors among the half-dozen or more men he had seen in the water after the keelboat had blown up. If so they had made their way out of reach of the Mandans during the past night.

It was noon when he saw the Indians returning, laden with salvage. They headed on upriver, passing by the bluff without interest. Later, in the dull light of a day that had grown chill and lowering, he saw canoes crawl onto the river's surface and cross to the north shore.

"The hunt's over," he said. "They're goin' back to their towns."

Fever burned in Jeanne Fitzhugh. At times she was beset by icy chills. Zack brought soaked cloths from the river to combat the fever, and firewood to warm her when she shook uncontrollably.

Zack doubted if she would make it through the night. He could see that Sera was also near the limit of endurance. She had been without rest or food for nearly twenty-four hours — hours of battle and near-drowning and of flight and the strain of imminent capture. Gauntness had already laid a shadow on her plump face.

She had plaited her hair in a long pigtail which hung down her back. This drew it tightly back from her forehead. Its golden color was already tarnished and Zack saw that at its roots the natural hue was dark, peppered with gray. It came to him that she must have been a dashing beauty in her youth, and that a great wealth of this remained, although now it might be called character.

She caught him appraising her. "Do I

look as terrible as all that?" she asked plaintively.

"How old are you, ma'am?" Zack asked.

"What a rude question. I'm in my late thirties."

"That's about what I figured," Zack declared. "I'd have said thirty-five, takin' into account the way you gals have of fixin' yourselves up to look younger'n you are."

"Thank you," she said. "You are truly a bare-faced liar, aren't you? An ingratiating one, I must admit."

She sighed. "All I need is a little sleep," she added. "Say about thirty-six hours of it. A session with a hairdresser and a new dress. I might look almost forty in the right kind of light."

She went on, almost as though it were an afterthought, "And I could stand a bite of food."

She watched Zack's expression. "I'm sorry I mentioned that," she said. "But food seems to be on my mind."

Zack nodded. "I've been frettin' all morning, recallin' all the grub I could have eaten an' didn't. There was a shindig at the Rocky Mountain House in St. Louis one time. Lasted for three days. Tables heaped high. Buffalo hump ribs, brown an' crisp an' sizzlin'. Turkey, duck, platters of smaller stuff like oysters, brought all the way from New Orleans on ice. I keep thinkin' about the eatables I've left on my plates in a lot of places."

Sera nodded. "I can't help recalling a restaurant on the Champs Elysées in Paris where they served the most marvelous filet, smothered in truffles, and with courses of clear broth and shrimps cooked in wine sauce, with —"

"Quit torturin' me," Zack groaned. "I could eat a full-grown ringhorn buffalo bull, right down to the hooves."

Sera ran her hands over her hips. "I could forgo a few meals no doubt, but not willingly. However, we have no choice."

She looked at Jeanne who lay stirring and muttering in her fever. "Whatever are we going to do?" she asked. For the first time she was near the breaking point.

Zack found himself patting her comfortingly on the shoulder. He was a little startled. What was coming over him, pitying a Fitzhugh?

He said roughly, "I'll be gone a little while. Keep the fire up. There's plenty of wood."

"Where are you going?" she asked, trying to be matter-of-fact.

"It's safe now to take a look around. I

spotted some wreckage from the keelboat lodged in the midst of brush under a cut-bank. The Mandans overlooked it. Might be something there we can use. Might even find a gun if we're lucky."

Jeanne Fitzhugh stirred and threw back an arm, tossing aside the petticoat that covered her. "They're coming!" she babbled. "They're coming!"

Zack bent over her. "Easy," he said. "You're safe here with us."

His voice always seemed to reach her and drive away the demons. She looked up at him, the fierce wildness dying in her eyes, reality returning to her.

"I was raving, wasn't I?" she murmured haltingly. "Dreaming. Awful dreams. I'll try to be quiet. Are — are they still out there? The Indians?"

"No. They've been gone for hours. They went back to their towns across the river. There's no danger from them now."

Sera tucked the scant covering back around the girl. "Rest now, Jeanne, darling. We've found a hiding place. It was an owl's nest."

Zack arose. "I better be goin' while there's still light."

A darkening thought seemed mirrored on their faces as he turned away. He could not interpret it. Its memory followed him disturbingly as he descended the bluff. It was as though they shared an acceptance of something they deemed inevitable — and fatal to themselves.

He made his way to where he had sighted the brush-hidden wreckage. It had been visible from the bluff, but now that he was at eye level it was a different matter. He finally located it, caught in a tangle of willows which could only be reached by wading to his shoulders through muddy water and swampy footing.

A portion of the deckhouse was lodged there along with a few planks and timbers. He sorted among these, half-swimming in the cold river. He located a cask. After he had strained and exhausted himself getting it to solid land he found that it contained vinegar, a prized bulwark against scurvy in the mountains but of little value to him at this moment.

He continued the search, and had better luck. He found two soaked blankets, wrapped around a cornshuck mattress. Also a buffalo robe. Captain Biggle's bed, he realized.

He came upon relics more grim. The bodies of two men. One was from the cordelling crew. The other was that of

Cotton, the mate. It was a gruesome task, but the clothes of the dead might mean life for the living. Zack stripped them, even to their heavy shoes.

He searched until darkness drove him from the river, chilled and shaking. He found no food nor anything that might reinforce his knife as a weapon.

He returned to the Owl's Nest carrying his treasures. He called out when nearing the crevice. Dropping into the hide-out, he paused, a trifle nonplussed. Sera had been lying beside her niece for the sake of warmth and mutual comfort, for the wounded girl was being shaken by another chill.

They were gazing at him without speaking. He saw surging emotion in both the fever-flushed face of Jeanne and the toil-dulled eyes of Sera. Gladness! Uplifting gladness!

They dropped their gaze suddenly as though wishing to hide this from him. Abruptly he understood. He knew now what had been in their minds when he had left them to make his search. They had never expected him to return. They had taken it for granted that he was deserting them, leaving them to make out as best they could while he attempted to save his own skin.

Nobody spoke for a time. Raging resentment burned in him. The truth was that until this moment the thought of abandoning them had not occurred to him. But now the temptation was there and it had been brought into the open through their own anticipation.

"Figured I'd do what a Fitzhugh lard eater would have done if it'd been me lyin' there with a hole in my brisket, didn't you?" he demanded roughly. "You expected me to weasel away by myself."

It was Jeanne who answered. "Nobody would have blamed you. In fact you are a fool for coming back. It will only make you feel that much worse when you do finally have to quit us. You will have to do that sooner or later, if you're to have any chance of getting out of this. We know that. You know it."

Zack hammered wet blankets against rocks to flirt water from them. It also gave him opportunity to beat out some of his own fury.

"See to it that the blankets and clothes are dried," he growled at Sera. "Lucky that some of this stuff belonged to a small man. They might come close to fittin' you women to cover your nakedness. The rest of it can be made to do somehow."

They eyed him for a time. "I still say you are a fool," Jeanne said tiredly. They asked no questions, but he was sure they suspected from where he had obtained the masculine garb.

He crouched close by the fire until he was dry and warmer. Darkness came. This he had been awaiting. He arose and carefully whetted the sheath knife. He grasped the rim of the crevice, preparing to vault to the top. "Keep the fire hot," he said to Sera. "Don't worry if I'm gone quite a spell."

Again it was Jeanne who spoke. She seemed stronger. For the moment at least she had emerged from the mists of pain. "You don't have to come back. You owe nothing to us. You've done a great deal already, fur thief. Thank you for everything."

"I'll be back," Zack said. "You know that."

She motioned to him to bend close. "Take Sera with you," she whispered. "She must not die because of me."

"I spotted elk in a thicket down there," Zack snapped. "I think they yard up there every night. That's where I'm goin'."

"Elk?"

He touched the knife. "We've got to get food somehow."

"But — without a gun . . . ?"

"It'll take big luck," Zack said. "And patience. And more luck."

"It will be dangerous. I've heard that a cornered elk can be terribly savage, particularly if it is wounded."

"Who told you about elk?" Zack asked, curious.

"I've talked to company agents and a few mountain men who came to see the sights of civilization and visited the office."

"The office? You mean the company office? But Angus Macleod said that —"

Her head came up. "Angus Macleod? You know him? Why he was one I listened to often. He told me many things about this country."

Zack stood above her, frowning. "You talked to Angus Macleod, the missionary? But he told me he had never laid eyes on J. K. Fitzhugh. Nor, as far as he knew, had anyone else."

A glint of laughter brightened her thinned face. "I was there. I was working as a clerk in the office of Uncle Paul Chalfant. I thought it best to learn something of the business I had inherited. Aunt Sera had decided that I had schooling enough to make a lady of me. So I badgered Uncle Paul into letting me work as his amanuensis under an assumed name. We kept it a secret from everyone, even Mr. Macleod."

She paused a moment, and he believed the amusement took on a deeper significance in her eyes. "Strangely, I called myself Jessica Smith," she went on. "I was another of the Jack Smiths. It is a name that pops easily into the mind when one needs another identity."

Zack's gaze was flat, without expression. He was thinking that if she had been that close to the operations of Fitzhugh Fur she must have known of its methods in the mountains.

"When was it you talked to Angus Macleod?" she asked.

"When?" Zack ransacked his mind. Time had meant nothing lately. Had it been only days since that moment, when, in his swaggering uplift of spirit, he had displayed his strength by tossing a log in the manner of the caber for the good missionary's admiration? Or had it been weeks? Or months?

"Not long ago," he said. "Ten days, maybe. Maybe less."

"Where was it?"

"Upriver," said Zack. "At Fort Jeanne."

"Perhaps we will see him there," she said hopefully. She added wanly, "That is — if we make it there ourselves."

"You'll make it," he said. He withheld the knowledge of Angus Macleod's death. Such news at this time could only be a burden upon her in her fight for strength.

He vaulted the rim of the niche. "I won't be far away. If you want me, toss a rock down the bluff. I'll hear it."

He was gone then, descending through the darkness down the rocky flank.

Jeanne lay listening, but no sound came back, not even the slightest scrape of a displaced pebble. She had previously noted this sinewy agility in him, this physical grace that offset the dominating effect of his height and brawn.

She let her thoughts run along that line, finding them comforting. He was equipped both by training and endurance for survival in this land in contrast to the inadequacy of herself and Sera.

She spoke out suddenly. "He despises us."

Sera drew a tired sigh. "I guess we've been thinking of the same things. But we can't expect a man who's been whipped to feel kindly toward us."

"It's true, isn't it?" Jeanne asked.

Sera hesitated. "What's true?"

"The things Angus Macleod told Uncle

Paul the company was doing in the mountains. The things we came here to find out for ourselves whether we were guilty or not."

"Now, don't go jumping to any wrong conclusions just because Jack Smith says so. Even if there was anything wrong, Paul has taken care of it by this time."

"By whipping men?"

"He probably got only the punishment he deserved," Sera said. "Likely he's no better than the Indians who tried to kill us. Sometimes I wonder if it wasn't him who brought them down on us. Maybe he was the one they were after."

Jeanne shook her head. "That doesn't seem possible, and you know it."

She lay silent for a time, and Sera hoped she had fallen asleep. But she spoke again. "Instead of him bringing the Mandans down on us, I had a terrible feeling that it was you and I they were trying to kill above all else. It seemed to me their fire was concentrated mainly on us at all times."

"I've heard soldiers who have been in battle say the same thing," Sera said. "It seems to be human nature to imagine that all of the enemy is shooting at you personally."

"I heard someone shouting orders on shore," Jeanne went on. "In English and in Indian language. A white man's voice."

"Now what are you imagining?" Sera protested. "Maybe there are white renegades among the Mandans."

"I had a feeling that the voice was directing the fire upon us," Jeanne said.

"You are having the vapors," Sera remonstrated. "Now don't waste your strength worrying. You need every bit of it."

"If Jack Smith dies, we all die," Jeanne said. "Jessica Smith dies, and also J. K. Fitzhugh. Why is he staying with us when he feels that J. K. Fitzhugh is responsible for his troubles?"

"Please try to sleep, dear."

"I believe I know who he really is," Jeanne said. "And I think you do too, Aunt Sera."

"There you go, imagining again!"

"It's not imagination," Jeanne said. "We've refused to face facts because we've been afraid. Some of this ugly talk we heard about the methods of Fitzhugh Fur in the mountains concerned two brothers named Logan who tried to start their own trading company two or three years ago. Angus Macleod spoke to Uncle Paul about them. One of the Logan brothers was drowned somewhere on the Missouri River."

"Now why go into that?" Sera protested.

"It's been on your mind as well as mine," Jeanne said. "I know you very well, Aunt Sera. The other Logan dropped out of sight. His name, if I recall correctly, was Zachary Logan. Angus Macleod described him one day when I pretended idle curiosity. My curiosity was not idle, I assure you. Angus Macleod's way of describing him was to say that Zachary Logan was tall enough to stand above the forest and strong enough to be gentle."

Sera clucked her lips scoffingly. "Bosh! What a description! And that's the reason you think he's —"

"Oh, I also learned the color of his hair and eyes," Jeanne said. "But they don't count. You aren't fooling me, Seraphine Clymena Fitzhugh. You too are sure he's Zack Logan."

"Even if he is, you don't imagine that he's going to chain us to a post and give us this twenty and one they talk about?"

"Maybe he thinks that won't be punishment enough," Jeanne said.

"You don't mean you believe he intends to do away with us?"

"He might be capable of it," Jeanne replied. "Living among wild animals and wild people would brutalize a man."

"They say that often such a life makes a person more merciful," Sera said. "Sometimes it brings out the best in humans."

"And sometimes the worst."

"If you're so sure you know who he really is, why don't you have it out with him?" Sera asked. "Put it to him, face to face."

Jeanne gazed wanly. "You know why. I'm afraid of the answer. And so are you."

Sera nodded tiredly. "You're right. I admit it. But I won't believe anything until we talk to your uncle. Paul will give us the truth. Whatever happened, it will be made right. So, missy, let the both of us keep quiet until we can talk to Paul and straighten everything out in our minds. As far as I'm concerned Jack Smith is Jack Smith until he wants to tell us something different."

"We're not only afraid of the answers," Jeanne said, "but we're afraid to face facts with him because we know we are completely dependent on him. If he leaves us, we will never survive to talk to Uncle Paul or anyone else."

"Maybe he won't come back this time," Sera said. "That will solve it for us. We would never have to face his answers."

Jeanne closed her eyes and sank into restless sleep. Sera placed more wood on the fire and turned the drying blankets so they would get full advantage of the heat. She wept a little. She tried to sleep, but succeeded only in listening to the silence of the night into which Zack had gone.

Hours passed. Abruptly the silence was broken. Faintly the echoes of a commotion in the brush below the bluff drifted through the darkness. The shrill whistling of stampeding elk arose, mingled with the frenzied bellowing of a bull. The crash of animals, running through the thickets, came. All of these sounds swiftly faded and silence returned.

Jeanne had aroused and lifted her head, listening. She and Sera looked at each other, not daring to voice the fear that was so poignant in their minds.

CHAPTER EIGHT

Zack inched his way along a game trail the elk had beaten in the brush. A light breeze was moving, its direction eastward, and he had circled downwind before entering the thickets.

Elk were near, and more were arriving, drifting in from the plains. The trunk of a huge cottonwood which had been carried by floodwaters of the past lay marooned in this lowland. Its rootbase poised it a few feet above ground, and a game trail passed close by it. It offered a spot on which to lie in wait in the hope his quarry would wander within leaping reach without scenting him.

He pulled himself onto the prone trunk and flattened out. The wait began. He could hear elk cropping at willows not far away. Presently one approached within a dozen feet. Another step or two and Zack would have leaped. But the animal, a dark shape in the starlight, shifted its course and moved out of range.

Time crawled by. The thin cold worked into his still-damp garb, and he began to shake. He clenched his jaws to still any betraying sound of chattering teeth. At times the grinding pain of cramping muscles forced him to shift position.

He accomplished any movement only at the expense of great effort, lifting each arm, each leg, each pound of weight so slowly there would be no sound. For the elk were well equipped for detecting danger even in the dark. The slightest error on his part would send them fleeing to the open plains for safety.

He knew that, at best, he would have only one chance and never another, at least in this place, for the elk were not likely to return to a spot where danger had once threatened.

He let his thoughts turn to Jeanne Fitzhugh and her aunt. At least they had never whimpered nor asked a favor of him. Jeanne must know that the odds were against her pulling through. She had rebounded from the first depths of weakness, but Zack had seen that happen before. She had lost a great amount of blood, and that would work against her when the greater reaction struck. What she needed now was nourishment. Without food she had no chance at all.

He remembered her courage as the knife

had probed into her flesh. And her beauty. Why had such a person ventured into the trapping country? Surely she must have been aware that she might encounter men like himself who had a score to settle with J. K. Fitzhugh.

Among mountain men the scriptural code of an eye for an eye prevailed. Zack was not the only one who had suffered at the hands of Fitzhugh Fur. Didn't she understand that all these matters were laid at the door of the owner? Once it was known that she was that person she stood a good chance of being the target of a bullet or a thrown knife from ambush. Vengeance in a matter of this kind would not be softened because of her sex. In fact the punishment inflicted might be all the more brutal and degrading because of that circumstance.

She was out of place in this land — a rose among cactus and tough buffalo grass. Even more incongruous was the presence of the opera-singing aunt. Seraphine Fitzhugh, of course, had faced the journey out of loyalty to her niece. Accustomed to the refinements of their sheltered lives, neither, Zack felt certain, had suspected that vengeance might be taken against them. Indeed, that vengeance might already have been attempted.

There were many puzzling aspects to the ambush of the keelboat. It had evidently been planned and carried out with a precision that exceeded the usual Indian ability. The careful way the Mandans had been deployed around the camp, the persistence with which they had followed up the first attack and had hunted down survivors, indicated a powerful directing hand. They had also seemed very well equipped with powder and lead — always scarce and precious.

Even the hour of attack — in complete darkness after nightfall — was contrary to Indian custom. In this case it had been a murderously excellent moment for such an assault, catching the keelboat party totally unarmed and outlined against the light of the fire.

If it had been engineered by someone out for vengeance on Fitzhugh Fur, that someone had possessed considerable backing. It would have taken not only vocal persuasion but material gifts in quantity to have prevailed on the Mandans to turn on the company with which they had been allied for so long.

This might explain the relentless way the Mandans had carried on the massacre. They had been determined that there be no survivors to tell tales.

All this could not have been the work of any mere grudge-bearing trapper. There were the other big fur companies, competitors of Fitzhugh, of course. But the era of bitter rivalry, of trap smashing and pitched battles, had ended years ago, and the other companies, to Zack's knowledge, were ethically operated. Furthermore, there were no competing agencies within two hundred miles or more. Some of the trading companies were no longer maintaining posts on the river but had adopted the plan of meeting the trappers each summer at various rendezvous in the mountains.

All of these suppositions came back to their starting point. The only plausible explanation seemed to be that it had been an act of treachery on the part of the Mandans. They might have seen a chance to loot a keelboat and been unable to resist the temptation. In that case their plan, no doubt, would be to see that their enemies the Rees or the Crows or even the distant Cheyennes were blamed. The fact they had gotten very little loot because of the destruction of the boat by fire and explosion, would be a sore point with them but, at least, they had taken scalps and counted many coups.

Zack kept thinking of the bateau he had sighted stealing down the far shore of the Missouri. The belief persisted in him that, whoever they were, the occupants of that craft had been involved in the massacre.

He quit thinking and concentrated on the matter at hand, that of attempting to down an elk. He found himself fighting off sleep. That was a real battle, as physically demanding as actual conflict.

Time after time his head drooped forward, and his chin would come in contact with the barkless trunk on which he lay. This would arouse him, and he would fight it out once again. Only the occasional approach of quarry kept him going. The elk were foraging steadily through the brush. At times all these sounds would become faint as the animals worked their way to a distance. On one occasion the thickets were silent for so long a time that he believed the band must have become uneasy and left permanently.

Just as he was about to give up, he heard them again. But it was a long, bitter wait before any grazed close enough to really revive his hopes. He guessed that the hour must be nearing midnight, or perhaps long past, for he could no longer judge time. Overhead the stars vanished, shut out by a thin overcast that was faintly luminous, catching the pale light of a dying moon.

An elk approached, moving indolently from one selection to the next. The animal was only a faint moving shadow.

Zack, gripping the knife, made ready, even though he held little hope, remembering other disappointments of the past hours.

This time the elk came nearer. It was a rod away, then half a rod. He could make out the silhouette of its antlers.

It was a full-grown bull. Zack had hoped for a cow or at worst a yearling. He had no choice. The elk was so near it must certainly discover him any moment.

That was what happened. The animal snorted, threw back its head and started to whirl. It had caught the alien scent.

Zack leaped. The distance was no more than six feet. He landed astride the animal's back, the knife lifted high. He had visualized this part of it during his long vigil and had mapped his method of attack. He had at first decided that he would attempt to slash the jugular vein, but had ruled against that. At this season the wintry coat would have thickened the stiff matt of coarse hair along the throats of the creatures, offering too great a problem for a weapon as inadequate as a knife.

The elk reared in an attempt to unseat him, its terrified whistle rising. He drove the knife downward, aiming at the spinal cord at the base of the skull, believing that this was the most vulnerable point at which he had a chance of success.

The animal's action had thrown him off balance. Nevertheless he felt the blade plunge deep. He tried to withdraw it for another stroke, but it resisted.

The elk whirled, and he lost his grip on the knife. He clung to his plunging quarry for a moment, desperately trying to regain the weapon. He failed. The elk spun violently and reared. He was flung loose and plunged to the ground at the beast's feet.

It attempted to slash him with its hooves, leaping and striking at him, bellowing loudly. A heavy blow raked his arm and that member went numb.

He rolled away, seeking escape. He felt the warmth of streaming blood, his own, he believed, for he feared that his arm had been laid open.

It was the trunk of the tree on which he had waited in ambush that saved him. He rolled beneath it where it stood propped on its roots and was out of reach of the frenzied bull. He huddled there, sheltered, while the animal slashed the brush to shreds nearby, still trumpeting its anger.

At last it turned and ran. The others of the band had already headed for the open plains. The roar of their flight was receding. Zack listened to the departure of the bull. He finally crawled shakily from his refuge and got to his feet.

His left arm dripped gore. He wrapped the torn sleeve of his shirt around it and climbed to the knob. He dropped heavily into the hideout.

Sera had kept the fire alive. She and Jeanne were awake. Jeanne was again flushed with fever. Her head lifted, and she stared wildly. It came to him how he must look, smeared with dust and blood.

"Good mercy!" Sera spoke, horrified. She was wearing a *voyageur*'s jacket over her dress and a pair of the heavy brogans Zack had brought from the river. It composed a very bizarre costume.

"I tried to fetch down an elk, but he was too much for me," Zack said. He added, with a tired gesture, "I even lost the knife. I got us in a worse fix than ever. I'm surely sorry." He sat down, his legs suddenly without strength.

Sera came to his side and examined his injured arm. The damage extended from

164

the shoulder half way to the elbow, but he saw that it was not much deeper than a painful scratch. He realized that some of the gore that smeared him must have come from the elk.

"I'll take off your shirt," Sera said. "I'll have to go to the river and soak some cloths to bathe that arm."

"I'll go," Zack said.

She pushed him back when he started to rise. She gently pulled off his shirt. "I doubt if you could make it," she said. "But I'm rested."

She ascended to the knob by way of the shallow narrow end of the crevice. She hesitated a moment as she faced the darkness. In the next moment she went off into the blackness, picking her way down the bluff toward the lonely river.

Zack found Jeanne's fever-darkened gaze fixed upon him. In her eyes was horror — and also a sense of defeat, as though she had finally been brought face to face with something she could not deny. He suddenly realized what it was. She was seeing for the first time the still-crimson welts of the half-healed whip marks on his back.

She said nothing. Her head sank back. Just as he had feared, she was losing ground.

"I lost the knife," he said again, self-condemnation tearing at him. "I ought to have held onto it."

Jeanne aroused. "Go away!" she gasped wildly. "Go away from this place, Jack Smith. Take Sera with you. Quit mocking me."

Sera came panting up the bluff and descended into the crevice carrying a dripping cloth. She had arrived in time to hear that outburst. "Stop it, dear," she implored.

Jeanne sank back and turned her face away from Zack. Sera bathed the wound on Zack's arm as best she could and formed a bandage. She moved to where Jeanne lay, smoothed back her hair and applied a damp cloth.

"She's worse," she murmured, returning to Zack's side.

"She needs food," Zack said. "And so do you."

He sat there, again thinking of that moment when the elk had tossed him aside and fled with the knife in its flesh. He kept telling himself that he should have been more careful. He should have made sure of his thrust. He should have hung on a moment longer and at least retrieved the knife.

Sera placed a hand on the back of his neck, massaging it and the sinews of his shoulders with the comforting touch of a woman. "Stop blaming yourself," she said. "If it is to be that way it is God's will."

She spread blankets for him where he would be helped by the reflected heat from the rock walls. "You must have some rest," she told him.

Zack fell asleep almost at once. Whenever he awakened he found the fire burning warmly. Sera was looking after it.

He slept through until dawn. He was finally aroused by a familiar sound in the distance. It was the barking and squabbling of coyotes. Against the gray wintry sky above he could see ravens circling.

He arose and gazed from the rim of the Owl's Nest. The brush where he had met disaster with the elk extended to a clay flood bank. Beyond that stretched the bunchgrass plains. Far to the south the plains broke into what seemed to be a collection of folded hills.

Near at hand, not far beyond the rim of the flood bank, a mottled gray object of some size lay in the bunchgrass. A dozen coyotes were circling, barking, and racing in occasionally only to retreat.

It was the bull elk. It had made it that far

in the darkness and there it had fallen, too weak to continue. Evidently it was still alive or the pack would have closed in.

Zack uttered a great shout. It awakened Sera and the sunken-eyed Jeanne. He ran down the bluff and through the brush to the plain. The coyotes retreated to a greater distance, yammering frenziedly.

The elk was breathing its last as Zack reached its side. It made one last noble effort to rise and thrust at him with its antlers. Then it expired.

The knife still jutted from its neck, almost hidden in the heavy mane. The blade had missed the spinal cord, but had dealt a death blow, nevertheless. It had penetrated deep enough so that the creature had succumbed to loss of blood.

Zack discovered that Sera had followed him. Between them they spent the day carrying meat to the hideout and holding the coyotes at bay. Gray wolves appeared. Ravens and magpies circled in swarms, darting in at every chance to peck at the carcass. But no human contender for the spoils — or for their scalps — appeared.

CHAPTER NINE

Zack and Sera broiled meat in the hideout. It restored their own vitality, but if Jeanne strengthened under the stimulus of the tiny morsels that Sera placed between her lips, the change was not apparent. She was almost too weak to swallow. When dusk came her link to life was very frail.

Dusk brought a new foe. A cold fingertip touched Zack's forehead as he emerged from the crevice for a last trip to salvage what he could of the carcass of the elk where the wolves had now moved in.

Snow!

He brought in the last of the elk and made another trip to replenish their supply of firewood. When darkness closed in the snow was sweeping over the knob, carried by a rising wind.

The plains winter had arrived. It was an opponent as savage as the Mandans and more relentless. This was its first blow, feeble compared to what lay in store during the winter months to come, Zack knew from bitter experience.

Sera gave him a tragic look and then did

not again let him see the thoughts that were in her. Jeanne had emerged from her lethargy. The occasional snowflakes which were blown under the overhang where she lay glistened on her flushed cheeks and vanished. She was rational, aware of the storm and of Sera's despair.

"Come to me, Sera," she murmured. Sera moved to her side. With a surge of strength Jeanne drew her aunt close and kissed her. "He'll get you out of this," she breathed. "I know that as surely as I know there's a mercy in heaven for us. Don't give up, Seraphine, my dearest aunt. He's strong. So strong."

Sera seemed to find solace and hope. She straightened. She was sobbing, but she conquered that. She brushed away the tears and tried to smile. "Don't waste your strength on me, darling Jeanne," she said. "You are so strong yourself. So very strong of spirit."

Jeanne spoke to Zack. "There will be no more tears. From either of us. We will not add things like that to your burden, Jack Smith."

The snow was still flooding down when daybreak came. Zack could have slept hours longer, but there was much to be done, and he was astir. He first brought rocks and built a smokehouse for the meat. Without salt, the smoked meat would be tough and tasteless but it would well sustain them. However, their larder had its limits, and there was little hope that he would ever get another chance such as the one in the brush.

On the other hand, the northern buffalo ranged these plains in winter. He had not seen any of these beasts since the day he had first encountered the keelboat but he was certain that they would appear again, sooner or later.

The storm had at least one advantage for them. It shielded their meat-smoking activities. It also covered any tracks they might have left. There was little chance any person, white or red would be about in this weather. Zack took advantage of all this and stored in a week's supply of firewood.

Jeanne lay thin and waxen. She was too weak to chew the elk meat Sera gave her.

Zack searched the bluff until he found a small flat slab of rock in which a hollow had been formed by weather action. This natural cup would hold less than a pint of liquid, and the vessel was unwieldy to say the least.

He and Sera heated it by the fire, accomplishing the task with infinite care and slowness, fearing that it would crack at any moment. But it remained intact. Once the rock was hot they added elk meat and water and let the result simmer for a time.

This broth Jeanne was able to swallow. Afterwards she fell into a motionless sleep from which Zack believed she would not awaken.

The snow turned to a driving rain. This was harder to endure than the snow, and Zack spent the greater part of the night out in it, building a rock barrier to protect the stricken girl's bed from the weather.

She was still alive at daybreak. No change came during the day, and the harsh rain beat down drearily. She still clung to life when dusk of the third day came. She hardly even knew Sera now, so weak had she grown.

There was nothing Sera could do except to spoon broth between her gray lips occasionally, using for this purpose a shaped section of willow bark which Zack had whittled.

The rain ended, but the weather remained overcast. Harsher days were in the offing, Zack knew. He watched Jeanne fight for life. He wanted to help her, but there was no way. He understood that only her own determination to live was keeping her going.

Each day and each night he hunted for game. The only result of patient hours of stalking or of lying motionless in cold vantage points was one small snowshoe rabbit which he killed with a thrown club.

Peering from the Owl's Nest early one morning he saw dark specks on the plains to the southwest which had not been there at dark. Buffalo. They were half a dozen miles away, at least, and perhaps farther. Judging distance in this light on the plains was a matter of guesswork.

He stalked them, hoping he might be able to down a calf or crippled animal with his feeble weapon. He spent a tense, freezing day at the task, but the buffalo grazed stubbornly in open flats which offered no cover for his approach. When at last, in desperation, he attempted to walk slowly up to them, knife in hand, the beasts scented him before he was within rods of them and stampeded away. He stalked them again and again with the same result. The herd, which totaled only some thirty or forty animals, grew wilder and more alert each time.

Darkness found him far from the Owl's Nest. It was long past midnight when he mounted the bluff, weary to the bone, and famished. The warmth of the firelit sanctuary reached out to him. Sera had meat broiling and broth steaming in the hollow rock.

She helped him out of the half-frozen blanket that he had wrapped around himself and knelt and removed the brogans from his feet which were more accustomed to moccasins. She treated the frostbite and blisters with lukewarm water which she kept heated in a receptacle she had improvised from a scrap of tarred canvas she had found among the wreckage of the keelboat, and which hung on a pole in the reach of the fire.

She again massaged the back of his neck, a ministration that seemed magically to ease weariness.

"Your medicine is good, ma'am," he said.

The fireglow reflected ruddily from the walls. He felt a tightness in his throat. Here, for the moment at least, was security after the loneliness of the plains.

He saw in Sera's face the brightness of released tension. He had witnessed this previously upon his return to the sanctuary after long absences, but on this occasion there was a greater gladness in her. Sera's

174

smile was radiant His glance swung to Jeanne.

Sera spoke in a whisper as though fearing words might break something frail and priceless. "Yes. She's better."

He moved to Jeanne and bent closer. She looked up at him, and the shadow of a smile showed. "I'm going to make it now, fur thief," she murmured. "It's high time I turned back, isn't it?"

There was no doubt about it. A new quality was in her voice, faint as it was. There was a small spark in the depths of her eyes as though some ember had been reached at last by a current of air and was springing into flame.

Yes, she had turned back on the dark path down which she had been drifting. Youth, vitality, the will to live — whatever it was — had swung the decision in her favor. Zack held her hand. In that moment she was not a Fitzhugh, but an indomitable young woman who had fought her own fight and had won.

"Yes," he said, and found that his voice was husky. "You've been playing possum long enough."

By morning there was no doubt that their patient was gaining. She was able to eat a little. Zack saw the first faint return of color in her throat.

He spent the day at the lookout. He sighted buffalo again, but they were miles to the west and drifting. He decided that it was the same herd that had eluded him the previous day. He knew it would be almost impossible to approach the animals on foot now.

His attention was centered mainly on the country across the river. The terrain beyond the Missouri was more broken than that of the near side. A thin line of brush marked a small watercourse which meandered in from broken hills.

More weather was near, for the lowering clouds had again closed in, forming a bleak roof. However, beneath that overcast the air was crystal clear, with visibility almost unlimited.

Zack was sure he saw a thin blue haze above the ridges beyond the river.

Jeanne spoke. "What is it you keep looking at, Jack Smith?"

"Smoke, I hope," he said. "North of the river. But not too far. A Mandan town, I'm sure. I didn't figure any would be close enough to be in reach."

"In reach?"

"We've got to raise us some kind of a weapon that'll be better than a knife," he said. "A rifle, above all. Or even a pistol would help. Maybe a bow and arrow. I could use them. I've had some practice at it — but not in earnest."

She and Sera suddenly understood what was in his mind. Sera framed a protest, then decided not to voice it. Jeanne was silent for a time. Finally she spoke as though accepting something inevitable. "The river? How will you cross?"

"On a raft," Zack said. "A float, rather. I won't need much. A few dry poles to help me long enough to make it. There's driftwood in the thicket, some of it dead enough and half punky so that it'll be easy to break and will float like a cork. Crossing won't be much of a problem."

"You should not try it."

"I'll make it easy," Zack said scoffingly.

"That isn't what I mean, and you know it. What happens after you cross?"

"If you stood in my place what would you do?" Zack asked.

"I'd — why I'd —" She had no answer. Zack shrugged. The matter was settled to his satisfaction at least.

The thicket, after considerable searching, yielded what he wanted — lengths of timber above sapling size, but dead and brittle enough so that he was able to break them into portions of no more than a dozen feet. He carried these to the river and used strips of elkhide and withes of soaked willow to bind six of them together. Testing them he decided that his craft, while treacherous, was sufficient for his purpose.

He returned to the sanctuary and slept until early darkness came, then arose and made his final preparations. He offered his knife to Sera, but she refused it. "You may need it much more than we," she said. "I can scratch and claw if necessary. I'm much better at it, in fact."

"Good girl," Zack said.

Jeanne spoke. "How long do you expect to be gone?"

"A day or two. Three, maybe." He hesitated. "If I'm not back in a week I won't be back at all."

She nodded gravely. "I understand. We can reach Fort Jeanne by following the river. Or is there a better way?"

Again Zack hesitated, then said, "Follow the river. It's farther, but you won't get lost."

"How far is it?"

"Depends," Zack said. "About four sleeps, I'd say."

"And how far is that in miles?"

"Well under a hundred. Maybe about eighty in a straight line, if you knew the country. Farther by river. But it's the weather you have to take into account. And you have to move slow and careful or you might bump into Indians who might be painted."

"I'll be able to travel any day now," she said.

Sera spoke. "We'll not be hasty about that, missy."

"We can't stay here much longer," Jeanne said. "We haven't seen real winter yet. Not the kind that will come. I've heard men talk of the bitter cold on these plains. And of blizzards that last for days. I doubt if we could make out in this crevice through the winter. We might freeze, not to mention the food problem. We may get snowed in here if we wait too long."

This same problem had been nagging at Zack. "We'll move out as soon as possible after I get back," he said.

"It will be so wonderful to see Uncle Paul again," she said.

"It will," Sera agreed fervently. "Heaven hasten the day."

"And Angus Macleod," Jeanne went on. "I do hope he is staying at the fort for the winter. I want to see his expression when he learns that I'm the prissy female clerk he talked to so many times at the company offices. He'll be more surprised when he finds that this Jessica Smith, whom he knew, is in the company of the Jack Smith whom he knows."

She eyed him challengingly and added, "Or does he know you by the name of Jack Smith?"

He saw that there was no longer any point in posing as something he was not, nor any purpose in keeping from her the truth about Angus Macleod.

"I have bad news," he said. "Angus Macleod has passed away."

"Passed away? You — you mean — dead?"

"Yes. I didn't tell you this before because it wouldn't have done you any good, hearing such news, weak as you were. He died at Fort Jeanne while I was there. I'm sorry. He was my friend."

Saddened, she was silent for a time. "He was a good man," she said. "He was partly responsible for our being here. Mainly responsible, in fact."

"In what way?" Zack asked.

She apparently had decided to confide in him. Or perhaps to face an issue that she had been evading. "One purpose of Angus

180

Macleod's trip east," she said, "was to talk to Uncle Paul about complaints in the mountains in regard to Fitzhugh Fur's supposed way of doing business. Rev. Macleod spent a great deal of time with Uncle Paul. They were old friends."

"What did your Uncle Paul do about these complaints?"

Zack's tone caused her to stiffen a trifle. "As a matter of fact, we had been hearing disturbing rumors of such things for some time before Angus Macleod's visit. Uncle Paul had already sent an order to the *bourgeois* at Fort Jeanne, Quinn Spain, to come east and explain."

"Just what was he to explain?" Zack asked.

"The complaints, of course. Another thing that was worrying Uncle Paul was the fact that the company has been losing money for the past three or four years. Not enough furs have been coming out of Fort Jeanne to pay expenses. The fur business is changing, of course, now that beaver is down, and that is the main trouble, no doubt."

"So it was money that brought you out here?" Zack asked.

She flushed. "Not entirely. However, we happen to know that other companies, like

181

American Fur, are still doing well."

Sera spoke, her feathers ruffled. "Are we right in assuming that you also are in the mountains for profit, young man? To earn money, in other words?"

Zack thought of his sables. Sera could see that she had scored a point. "Ha!" she said. "I see that you have your mercenary side, along with the rest of us."

"Money was not the main reason why Uncle Paul came to the mountains," Jeanne said. "It does not matter to me whether you believe that or not, but it is the way it is. However, with beaver not profitable, there is a growing market for other furs. Uncle Paul feared a repetition of what was happening to beaver. They were growing scarce when the change in the style of men's hats came. That may have saved them from extinction. Uncle Paul got together with other reputable trading companies. After much bickering they adopted a system that would avoid what had almost happened to beaver. All fur was to be taken under a set plan, super-vised by a committee of members from all the companies in the agreement. No spe-cies was to be exploited beyond its ca-pacity, so that a constant crop of pelts could be taken each year."

"A good plan," Zack acknowledged. "In fact, there was something like that in the minds of —"

He broke off. Jeanne eyed him. "What were you going to say?" she asked.

"It doesn't matter," he replied.

The fact was that he and his brother had intended to propose a somewhat similar agreement when they had first formed their own trading company.

"It is a good plan," he repeated.

Sera joined in the conversation. "It *was* a good plan."

"You mean it didn't work?"

Jeanne answered. "It never had a chance. It was in effect only a season or two before other companies began complaining that Fitzhugh Fur was not keeping its word. They protested to Uncle Paul that our trappers were stripping the country of fur. They claimed all sorts of things — that their trappers had been robbed and that some of the tribes, particularly the Mandans, who have always been Fitzhugh friends, have been put up to making war on them."

"So that's why your uncle called Quinn Spain east," Zack said.

"Mr. Spain has been manager at Fort Jeanne for half a dozen years," she said.

"Uncle Paul has complete confidence in him. Mr. Spain denied the accusations. He said the truth is that Fitzhugh Fur is the one who is being preyed upon by the other companies. That's why our fur business has dropped off."

"And did you and your Uncle Paul believe him?"

"He has been with Fitzhugh Fur for years. He started with the company almost as a boy, clerking in the St. Louis agency. He has worked himself up. He and Uncle Paul have been personal friends. I was much impressed by him. I had never seen him before. He is a fine-looking man."

"I was more'n impressed by him," Zack said tersely. "I've still got the scars."

"Uncle Paul believed Mr. Spain," she went on. "But, about that time, Angus Macleod arrived from the mountains and supported some of the things that were being charged against Fitzhugh Fur. Mr. Spain defended himself strongly. He said that the minister was being used as a tool by the opposition. As a matter of fact, Reverend Macleod admitted that he had no actual firsthand evidence, but was only relating what other men had told him."

"Sort of put you and your Uncle Paul at the fork of the road without a map, didn't it?" Zack commented.

"In a way. We could hardly discredit Angus Macleod, nor did Uncle Paul want to doubt the word of our own agent. There seemed to be only one way of deciding the matter. Uncle Paul came to the mountains with Quinn Spain so that he could look into it personally."

"But I understand that they came in a year ago last summer," Zack said. "Why is Chalfant still at Fort Jeanne?"

"He was to have spent last winter there, of course, and intended to return to the headquarters office this past summer. But we received word by the first boat down-the Missouri last spring that he would not be able to make it until fall. Apparently he was unable to do that and is forced to stay over through another winter. I suppose he found the problem more difficult than he had anticipated. Distances are so enormous. It has been a mistake, maintaining the main offices in the east, now that the trapping business is in the far west. Uncle Paul had already made arrangements to shift the headquarters to St. Louis. I will make my home there in the future."

"But right now you came up the Missouri to do some investigating in person," Zack commented.

She again smiled, a trifle ruefully. "Yes. A woman's whim, I suppose. Or a woman's foolishness."

"Or maybe to see what Chalfant was up to," Zack snapped.

She gazed grimly at him but refused to lose control of her temper. "If Uncle Paul has met difficulties, it is my responsibility also," she said. "I don't intend to let him and Aunt Sera carry my burden any longer. That's why I decided to come to Fort Jeanne. The only reason. Poor Sera. We were on our way to Pittsburgh before she had a chance to think."

Sera bristled. "Don't you 'poor Sera' me. I was the one who encouraged you to come, if you want to know the truth. And right now, I feel twenty years younger to see you so pert and sassy."

Jeanne squeezed her aunt's hand. "We knew it was too late to catch the company's last keelboat carrying supplies to the post so we sent word ahead by fast post to our office at St. Louis to arrange a trip for us on a later, smaller boat. It is my duty to help Uncle Paul."

"Or to find out if he's in cahoots with Spain in robbing you," Zack said.

Her voice rose a trifle. "I'll never believe that."

Sera chimed in. "You've got no right to say such things about a man like Paul Chalfant, Jack Smith."

"My name," Zack said, "is Logan. Zachary Logan. My brother was Dan Logan. Maybe you've heard of Logan Brothers Fur?"

"Yes," Jeanne said exhaustedly. "I've been very sure who you really were since the very first night when you were caught aboard the keelboat."

"I've had a hunch you knew who I was," Zack said. "It puzzles me. You've never seen me before, to my knowledge. How did you guess I was Zack Logan?"

"One reason why Uncle Paul called Quinn Spain east was to explain ugly stories we had heard about open warfare between our company and a new company called Logan Brothers Fur. I discovered that Angus Macleod knew the Logan brothers personally. He described you to me."

"And what did Spain tell your good uncle about the Logan brothers?" Zack asked curtly.

"He said you two were the leaders of a pack of renegades and toughs who robbed and pirated, preying on other companies, principally Fitzhugh Fur. He said it had been necessary to meet violence with violence."

She paused a moment. "The latter statement has always been true of Fitzhugh Fur. We strike back when struck. Harder."

"Did Quinn mention that he was responsible for my brother being drowned?" Zack demanded.

Sera tried to intervene. "This is doing you no good, Jeanne, darling. Please go away, Zachary Logan. You'll give her a set-back."

"I'm sorry," Zack exclaimed. "We'll talk this over some other time."

Jeanne would have none of that. She was not giving in to weakness. In fact she seemed to have strengthened on the exchange. "We'll talk it over now. Quinn Spain said your brother was drowned when a keelboat was wrecked. It was an accident."

"It was no accident," Zack said. "The boat was cut adrift. Was it also an accident when Spain had a trapper friend of mine whipped at the post as a warning to me because he couldn't get his hands on me personally at the time? Was it an accident when he finally did catch me and give me the whip? And your uncle Paul Chalfant was there personally when they swung the lash."

"If Uncle Paul had you whipped, then you must have deserved it!" she said.

"And did your uncle and Quinn Spain deserve the twenty thousand dollars' worth of sables they stole from me?"

"Sables?"

"Siberian sable," Zack answered. "Pelts that I spent two years getting. I brought them all the way from the northwest coast over the big mountains. Chalfant and Spain robbed me of them at Fort Jeanne. They turned me afoot to starve or be scalped on the plains. They gave me a worthless rifle, sand for powder, pebbles for bullets, and a broken knife."

Her head sank back on the pallet. She stared at him drearily. Sera was sobbing, the tears bright on her cheeks.

"I can't believe it!" Jeanne said, her voice shriveled.

Zack turned away. "The sables I intend to get back," he said. "From Paul Chalfant or from Quinn Spain. With a whip, if necessary. With a gun, if needed. With a knife, if they want it that way."

He left the sanctuary. The knob faded into the background of stormy sky as he descended the bluff and was lost.

He found his raft and pushed it away from the bank. Presently the craft was taken by the current into deeper water, and he used the pole as a sweep, forcing it slowly toward the far shore.

The river was swollen by the rains. His craft was cranky and required precise balance on his part. Any wrong move caused it to roll dangerously, so that he was often immersed to his knees and facing capsizing in midstream. The icy water was an agony at first, but soon he was only numbed and weakening.

The raft was unable to withstand the buffeting of the current as he fought his way nearer the opposite shore. It broke up when he was almost in the shadow of the dim, dark line that marked safety. He found himself in deep water, swimming sluggishly and near the end of his strength.

He was thinking of Dan, who must have died like this, when his feet touched mud bottom. He floated and crawled through shallow water toward that dim shadow. When he finally pulled himself onto firm land he was completely spent.

He leaned against a leafless willow, not daring to sit or lie down for fear his numbed muscles would stiffen and never lift him to his feet again. After a time he revived and was able to move. That helped quicken circulation. His soaked garb was like an armor of ice, but even that seemed to ease considerably as he warmed to the pace.

From the knob he had studied the country carefully, mapping it in his mind. He judged that he had been carried nearly a mile downstream during the crossing. He retraced this lost distance, following the course of the Missouri until he could make out the black shape of the bluff across the river against the clouds.

With that as his guide point he turned away from the stream. Excitement buoyed him, and he covered ground speedily. In addition, his objective was much closer than he had estimated. In less than an hour after leaving the river he crossed a low divide and saw the glow of fires far ahead. A Mandan town.

He advanced and at last crouched on a rise near the outskirts of the community. The hour was still early, and the place was very active. There were only a score or so of the odd, round, dome-roofed houses built of logs and mud that were the hallmark of the Mandan.

Zack had expected much more than this. A deeper crimson tinge of firelight beyond the next rise gave him the answer. The village at which he was gazing was only an off-shoot of a larger Mandan town.

Frost-withered fields flanked the village where corn, beans, and other crops had been raised. The Mandans looked down on the nomadic tribes that ranged the land, dependent on the buffalo for existence. The Mandans were hunters too, but they fattened in winter from their storehouses while the Crows and Rees were starving in their lodges on the plains.

Zack crawled across one of the cultivated fields until he was looking directly into the village at close range. The Mandans boasted that they were also great warriors when the need came. Evidently the need had come the night the keelboat had been ambushed. In the glare of the fire that blazed high in the council circle Zack could see scalps hanging from poles in front of the lodges. Some of these trophies were in the lighter shades — brown, sandy, blond. White men's scalps.

The Mandans were leaving the houses and gathering in the central circle to take part in the nightly entertainment that was customary in Indian communities.

They were still making the most of the keelboat fight. It would be a topic of interest for months. A young brave had the center of the stage at the moment and was strutting around, waving a pole to which a scalp was attached. He was elaborating on his part in that affair. This, perhaps, was his first chance to gain attention after the older warriors had held forth each night in the interminable coup counting.

Someone began tapping on a drum. Young Mandan girls, blankets held above their heads, started to shuffle their feet in an invitation to the dance and as a hint to the braggart to end his monologue.

Some of the men, and the squaws too, wore red shirts and capotes and the striped breeches that Zack recognized. Loot from the bodies of slain keelboat men or from the stores of the *Jeanne Kathryn Fitzhugh* which had floated ashore.

He was perplexed. The Mandans were bold enough about it, displaying openly the rewards of their victory over Fitzhugh Fur. It destroyed one theory he had held, which was that the ambush had been an act of treachery. The only reasonable explanation now seemed to be that the Mandans had become enemies of the company instead of allies.

He worked his way closer, crossing the muddy mounds of a harvested bean field. If the Mandans were at war with anyone, they did not seem to fear attack, for there were no signs of sentinels. His biggest concern, for the moment, appeared to be possibility of discovery by the dogs of the village. However, the canine population seemed to be enjoying the warmth of the council fires, for he was undisturbed.

Half a dozen of the Mandan houses were clustered around the council area, but the remainder were scattered loosely in accordance with the ease of construction sites and convenience to a small stream, whose trees showed beyond the community.

Zack singled out the house which seemed to best serve his own purpose. It stood some fifty yards from its nearest neighbor and twice that distance from the council fire. He had seen a blanket-wrapped Mandan emerge from it and walk to the circle where he was given a place of honor. The house, by its size, was evidently the dwelling of a man of importance and was therefore likely to contain more material possessions than its neighbors.

He waited. Soon, a young Indian and a still younger girl left the house and hurried to the scene of entertainment. A minute or two later a fleshy squaw followed them.

No sound came from the house. Impatience drove Zack. There was every reason to believe the structure was deserted, but that chance might be short-lived. He moved in that direction, flanking the village, and wormed his way to the rear wall of the house. He pressed an ear against the logs, listening.

He could hear nothing, but the wall was solidly chinked with mud and built of strong logs. The silence was no positive assurance that the place was unoccupied.

He moved around the structure and, lying flat, peered out. The area seemed deserted, but the council circle was more noisy and active.

The house had a low sub-doorway, which served as a storm entrance. Zack crawled to this opening and scuttled through it. A buffalo robe hung over the main inner door. He pushed this aside and stepped in, straightening, the knife in his hand.

A fire, down to red coals, glowed in the central pit, laying a crimson radiance over the circular interior. A copper kettle hung over the pit.

The first object Zack's eyes picked out was a rifle which lay on pegs in the wall. A powder horn and shot pouch, attached to a shoulder belt, hung there with it.

He took an eager stride toward it. He had been lucky. The house seemed vacant.

He was wrong. A voice spoke impatiently

in English, "Who is it?"

A man was lying on a pallet of buffalo robes in the far reach of the room. He was barely visible in the uncertain light. He held a drinking horn. Zack caught the odor of rum.

With him was a young Mandan woman. She had been sitting beside the pallet, and it was evident that Zack had intruded upon an ardent moment. The man had not yet bothered to lift his head to look toward the doorway.

The young squaw turned. She was framing an angry order, but it changed to a frown of uncertainty as though she could not decide whether he might not have a right to be here.

The man aroused and came to a sitting position, twisting round to look. He was Quinn Spain!

The explanation of the squaw's hesitation flashed into Zack's mind. Some of Spain's men must be here in the village also, and the woman had wondered if he was one of them.

In any event that momentary reprieve gave Zack the advantage. He was moving. He had snatched the rifle from its place as Spain turned, for it was the nearest weapon in sight.

He was upon Spain before the man could move or even draw a breath to shout.

"Spain!" he gritted. "Spain!"

He smashed the butt of the rifle into Spain's face. He heard teeth grind, heard Spain's wheeze of agony. He remembered his own pain under the whip and he felt a savage surge of satisfaction.

The blow pitched Spain flat on the pallet, the wheezing continuing, and joined by a bubbling gasping effort.

The squaw screeched, but it was a thin effort from lungs shocked by fright. She scrambled frenziedly to the hearth and seized up a hatchet — a wicked weapon, useful in both war and in preparing game for the cookpot.

Before she could frame another outcry Zack was upon her. This was no time for observing decorum in regard to her sex. She was no delicate flower. She was young and handsome, but she was also solid-boned, solid-fleshed. In her daily duties she could carry burdens that would stagger many a man. She could skin and dis-member a buffalo, and could pack a travois and travel with it for miles, and finish out with an all-night stomp dance.

She could split a man's skull with the

hatchet as easily as she could decapitate a pet puppy for the cookpot. Zack had no room to raise the rifle and use it as he had on Spain. He had to silence her instantly.

His only effective weapon was his own head. His momentum carried him inside the arc of the hatchet as she came to her feet and swung savagely. The blow was ineffective. His head caught her in the stomach, and he carried her onward with him in two plunging strides that drove her against the wall with an impact that smashed the breath from her.

She slid to the floor, her face twisted in agony. Zack towered over her a moment, the butt of the rifle poised, for he was thinking of a scalp with long, sorrel-red hair which hung before this house. Big Louie, he of the light-hearted bluster on the cordelle, had possessed just such hair. This Mandan girl, no doubt, had carried it proudly aloft for whomever from this lodge had counted it among his coups at the council fire.

However, he withheld the blow. She was helpless, doubled on the floor, gasping in pain. The damage she had sustained would not be lasting, but she would be out of action for several minutes at least.

He whirled on Quinn Spain. Toward this

one he held even less compassion. Furthermore, the man offered a greater immediate danger. Spain lay on the pallet, hands clasped to his damaged face, blood flowing. But he was recovering already.

"I should stamp you to death," Zack said.

All that he could bring himself to do, however, was to raise the rifle again and ram it violently into Spain's stomach. And that blow was an act of precaution and not of vengeance.

It left the man gagging and gasping for breath in much the same condition as his savage paramour.

From the council circle the hi-yah chant of the squaws continued unbroken, along with the swish of the shuffle dance.

Zack buckled on the powder horn and pouch. They and the cap box seemed to be amply supplied. The rifle evidently had belonged to the Mandan who was head of this household. It was battered, but in fair condition as Indian rifles go, and there was a charge in it, with only a cap needed for the nipple. This Zack supplied. The weapon's stock was decorated with big brass tacks, set in the owner's medicine sign. It carried half a dozen knife-cut notches — the tally of coups over enemies, or over the grizzly bear, an opponent more dangerous even than a human in tribal estimate. A scalp, a memento of one of those notches, was tacked to the underside of the stock. It was an Indian's hair.

The pallet on which Spain lay paralyzed and doubled up was covered with a fine six-point blanket. Zack snatched this up, dumping Spain bodily on the floor alongside the writhing squaw.

A sizable storage gourd stood near the fire, filled with parched corn. A roll of pemmican lay on a chopping block. He placed these on blankets. He emptied the copper kettle of the meager remains of a stew and added the receptacle, still hot, to his collection.

He delved into the recesses of the room. The area where the squaws carried on their garment-making activities yielded treasures. He found a pair of new elkhide leggings that evidently had been intended for the young Mandan he had seen emerging from this house, as well as a calfskin vest and two pairs of moccasins, one set of which might even fit him.

His next discovery was a quiver of arrows, some of which were heavy shafts for buffalo or other big game, along with a hunting bow. He added another blanket and a buffalo robe and a squaw's waist of blue strouding and two petticoats.

He descended on Spain. The man was clad in fine mackinaw breeches, a warm flannel shirt, and stout, high-topped moccasins. Zack stripped them from him, leaving him naked.

This gave him another idea. He eyed the squaw. She was wearing a gay beaded smock of soft fawnskin and low moccasins. He divested her of these garments as he would peel an onion. She had on nothing beneath the smock. He left both of his victims raw naked and gasping.

He placed the hatchet in his belt. It seemed to him that he must have been in this place for hours, although he knew that in reality it had been less than five minutes. He thought of tying and gagging the pair, but he sensed that he had pushed his luck, and that further delay would mean discovery.

He looked down at Spain for a moment, frowning. The man's presence here exploded the latest explanation he had settled on for the attack on the keelboat. If it had been an act of treachery on the part of the Mandans, Spain would hardly be here on friendly terms with them. Nothing added up.

He slung his booty over his shoulder in a blanket pack, crawled through the low entrance, and peered out. The dance was still going on. His way was still clear.

He raced away across the barren fields, heading toward the river. The chant of the dancers became fainter.

Suddenly that ceased. He could hear the high sound of shouting. He ran faster. His visit had been discovered.

CHAPTER TEN

After a time Zack veered eastward, keeping the river well to his right. There would be pursuit, but it would not likely pick up his trail until daylight. He moved fast. On the downhill slopes he broke into a lope. He wanted, above all, to lead the Mandans away from the vicinity of the bluff across the river.

His spirits were soaring, lifted by the success of the raid. The pack slung over his shoulder was the most precious possession he had ever held. In comparison the sables that Spain and Paul Chalfant had seized from him faded into insignificance.

He kept puzzling over Spain's presence in the Mandan village. The comely Indian girl was the easiest explanation, but Zack felt that it was not the right one. It did not seem reasonable that the *bourgeois* of Fort Jeanne would risk his prestige because of an infatuation with a woman of a tribe that had turned against the company he represented.

It was customary for fur-company agents to pay formal visits to tribes with which they traded. Normally, this could account for Spain's presence. But this was not a normal instance. Scalps of Fitzhugh Fur *voyageurs* were hanging in this particular village. Spain could not have overlooked these trophies of battle. Of massacre, rather. That had not been a battle but a ruthless slaughter.

There was, of course, the possibility that the Mandans had ascribed the scalps to some other feat. It was no secret that the Sioux tribes of the upper plains were at grips with white settlers to the east who were pushing farther and farther across the upper Mississippi River into the hunting grounds of the plains Indians.

Mandan war parties ranged far afield at times and sometimes brought back scalps that were not the black hair of traditional enemies such as the Blackfeet to the west or the Rees and Crows to the south. To wink at such things as long as their own interests were not damaged would be characteristic of Spain and the policy he had carried out in the name of J. K. Fitzhugh.

But there were puzzling circumstances that did not fit in with any of these possibilities.

Zack paused occasionally to rest. He shaved off scraps of the pemmican, which was almost as hard as wood, and as bitter of taste, but contained great nourishment. He would swing ahead again each time, ignoring the fatigue that crept through him.

After midnight he curled up in a bed of leaves and slept for two hours. He arose before daybreak and set out once more. At sunup he judged that he was more than twenty miles from the Mandan town. He veered toward the river and, when he reached it, searched along its margin for material for a raft. But on these treeless plains opportunity was scant.

It was noon before he found a patch of stranded driftwood on the outward swing of a bend in the river. Some of the thongs he had seized with his other loot in the Mandan house were of buffalo leather and would serve as lashings, but he was forced to sacrifice part of one blanket, ripping it into strips with his knife as reinforcement in case the hide lashings stretched too much when soaked.

He had no time or strength to build more than a rude float of four long, corklike cottonwood poles. It supported his loot, but he could only lie flat upon it, his body partly immersed as his weight sank the contrivance to water level. He kicked his feet for motive power and also awkwardly wielded a pole.

However, the river, though wider here, was quieter, and his craft held together. He knew that the point of his embarkation would doubtlessly be found by trailers before the day was over. He worked his way out from shore and let the current carry him downstream for two hours or more.

He could endure the cold no longer and propelled his raft toward the south shore. He drifted until he found a landing place of hardpan that would show no tracks. He stood in shallow water, dismantled his raft, and set the pieces adrift. He took great pains to leave no trail as he left the river.

Before dusk came he was on higher ground. He sighted canoes on the river and saw the smoke of signal fires on the north shore. The search was being carried on by land and water.

After dark, the help he had hoped for and which had been holding off all day finally arrived. Snow. It sifted down hard and gritty, for the temperature had plunged.

He located a dry covert in the lee of rocks and built a fire of small twigs and animal chips which he found there. It smoked considerably but also gave warmth. He dried his clothes somewhat, though they retained a persistent chill dampness. Some of his loot had been soaked in the river also during the crossing, but the food and ammunition were still protected.

He ate some of the pemmican. He extinguished the fire and moved to a new hiding place more than a mile away, not risking the chance that searchers might have come near enough to have detected the smoke. He built no fire here. He slept until well after daybreak, chilled and restless, but claimed by exhaustion.

It was still snowing when he awakened. A bitter wind was sweeping the flats clear, building drifts in the lee of the swells.

He set out, the storm shielding him and covering any trail he made. The snow ended toward midday, but the wind increased in strength, carrying drift with it and striking with a fury that would hold him, crouched and fighting for breath, for what seemed ages.

He circled well to the south of the bluff. He found a shelter place at midafternoon and waited there until dusk, watching his back trail. No sign of pursuit appeared. He began to believe he had shaken them off.

It was long past dark when he approached the bluff. A dreary fear entered him as he climbed. It seemed to him that there could be no such silence from above if they were still there.

It was not until he was very near the knob that he caught the tang of woodsmoke and saw the glint of firelight. He called out and felt a great upward surge of spirit when Sera's voice responded.

He dropped into the crevice, gleefully swinging his blanket-slung pack. "Santa Claus is ahead of time this year," he said.

Jeanne was propped in a sitting position near the fire, wrapped in a blanket. It was evident that she had continued to strengthen. There was now no doubt about the play of color in her throat. It had risen higher and was touching her cheeks. She was looking at him with bright joy.

Sera rushed to him, in tears, and threw her arms around him. "We're so glad you're back," she chattered. "So thankful."

Zack said, "Now, don't take on like that. I always show up. You must know that by this time."

Sera drew back, dabbing at her eyes. Zack opened his pack and began laying out the treasures. Sera seized up the copper kettle with a delighted scream. She uttered chuckling sounds of bliss when she saw the gourd of corn and the pemmican.

The blankets and the garment brought

squeals of wonder from both women. Jeanne looked at Zack and said, "Thank you. Now tell us about it."

In this moment there was only the knowledge among them that they now had a real chance for survival. All differences were put aside.

"Not much to tell," Zack said. "I just went into a Mandan house at night while they were dancing and helped myself."

She reached out and lifted the rifle. Zack had forgotten the scalp that hung from the stock. She realized what it was. She started to place the weapon hurriedly aside, then forced herself to retain it. She had noticed something else that had aroused her interest. She held the weapon near the firelight, peering closely at the shoulder rest.

"It looks like blood," she said quietly. "And a few short strands of hair. It could be red hair." She looked up at him. "Or brown, perhaps. At least it isn't black, like that of an Indian."

Zack remembered Quinn Spain's clipped mustache. He shrugged. "I bumped into a squaw man in the Mandan house. I had to lay him out with the rifle butt."

She indicated the smock and moccasins he had taken from the young squaw. "They look useful. A little gaudy perhaps."

"I figured the dress would be about your size."

"It will probably fit Sera better, at least until I get back a few lost pounds," she said, smiling. "How fortunate you found such an article. Where do Indians keep such things in their wigwams?"

"Mandans live in houses," Zack explained. "Oh, they hang staff around on pegs or whatever's handy, or pack it in parfleche bags and pack sacks."

She eyed him thoughtfully. "Are you sure it wasn't being worn at the time you found it?"

Zack ran his hand helplessly over his chin, and was shocked by the silky length of his beard. "I must look like a porcupine," he said. "I'll whack some of the fur off me tomorrow."

Zack was glad she had not shown curiosity about the squaw man. The amusement had enlivened her. She lay fingering the smock, studying him while Sera bustled around, broiling elk meat and concocting a stew of parched corn and pemmican.

"We'll be able to start for Fort Jeanne in no time at all," she said.

Zack said nothing. He was beginning to

understand that he could not let her or Sera go to Fort Jeanne until some things were explained.

CHAPTER ELEVEN

Jeanne's improvement was rapid. But she still overestimated her strength. After two days she insisted on dressing and getting on her feet.

Sera came to Zack for advice. He shrugged. "Let her find out for herself," he said.

Later, he watched the experiment. Sera, who considered masculine attire shocking, clung to her petticoats, and had commandeered the smock Zack had brought from the Mandan town. Jeanne, however, decided that the men's garb Zack had accumulated would be more practical and warmer. She arrayed herself in *voyageur* breeches, Quinn Spain's linen shirt, which was many sizes too large, the calfskin vest, and a pair of moccasins. As an impish gesture of jauntiness, she pulled on the Mandan leggings also.

She rolled up the sleeves of the linen shirt, bringing her hands into view. "Stand aside," she said.

She had never voiced curiosity as to the identity of the squaw man Zack had mentioned. Her silence in that respect caused Zack to suspect that she knew — or feared — the answer.

She waved aside Sera's offer of assistance and got to her feet confidently. From that point on it was a different story. She found her legs uncertain, her knees trembling. She managed to stagger shakily to the rock wall and lean against it. She saw that Zack was watching her. She did her best to straighten and move gracefully. It was a dismal failure. She was glad to return to her pallet and collapse upon it.

However, before the day was over, she repeated the experiment, and with a little more success. The following day she walked the length of the crevice and back without once depending on the walls for support.

She was triumphant and began badgering Zack to set an immediate date for their departure for Fort Jeanne. Fort Jeanne was on her tongue constantly. It was the mecca, the haven of safety, the goal where all anxieties and misunderstandings would be ended.

After another day or two she could contain her impatience no longer. "We will start tomorrow," she said flatly.

She blazed into anger when Zack shook

his head. "You're only being pig-headed!" she cried.

"Damned if I want to have to pack you on my back all the way to the Little Buffalo!" he exclaimed.

She stared at him. "The Little Buffalo? Isn't that the name of a river that flows into the Missouri quite a long distance downstream? Why, of course it is. Hank Gratt told me its name when we passed its mouth aboard the keelboat. Fort Jeanne isn't in that direction."

Zack had let the wrong name drop. The truth was that up to that moment he had not known for sure in his own mind that he had made this decision.

She was pinning him with a suspicious stare. Sera was gazing apprehensively at him also. "I don't think that you — we ought to try for Fort Jeanne," he said lamely. "Not soon, at least."

"Why not?" The animation had faded out of Jeanne. She must have seen something in his face that aroused dread in her.

"I have a friend who lives with the Crows," he said. "He told me their village would be camped for the winter on the headwaters of the Little Buffalo. It should not be hard to find. It might be wise to stay with him until you're stronger. He's a mountain man named Belzey Williams. He's got two Crow wives."

He laughed hollowly. "Two wives, poor fellow. He has his troubles, I suppose, without us adding to them."

Jeanne did not respond to his sad attempt at levity. "You want to take us farther from Fort Jeanne," she said accusingly.

"It won't be any farther," he said. "We'll cut south and strike the Little Buffalo a long ways west of where you passed its mouth. It might even be closer to the fort."

She was silent for a space. "What is the real reason you don't want us to go to Fort Jeanne?" she finally asked grimly. "Something happened the night you raided the Mandan house. I've always known that you didn't tell us everything."

"The warriors from that village were in on the massacre of the keelboat crew," he said. "I saw scalps, and I saw clothes that could not be mistaken."

She stood straight and pale. Sera uttered a small, sighing sound but did not speak. Both of them waited, and he saw that they were desperately afraid of what he was going to say next.

"The man whose blood you noticed on the rifle I brought back wasn't exactly a squaw man," he told Jeanne.

She must have remembered the few strands of hair that she had noticed on the butt of the weapon, for he was sure she had guessed what his answer would be before she asked the question. "Who was he?"

"Quinn Spain," he said. "Your agent at Fort Jeanne."

The new color left her still-thin features. "Do you know what you are saying?" she asked. "You're saying that one of our own people must have had a hand in sending that raid down on us. That's impossible! Why would Quinn Spain do a thing like that?"

"Maybe because you were aboard."

She was ashen now. "Go on."

"Maybe Spain didn't want you to reach Fort Jeanne," Zack said. "Maybe he didn't want to have to explain a lot of things such as why Fitzhugh Fur has not been showing a profit and why it has violated all the rules of decency in the mountains."

"You're trying to tell me that he wanted me dead," she said. "Murdered. Do you know what that means? Do you know that you are as much as saying that they killed all those men in the crew so that nobody would live to tell what happened. Samuel Hunter too. Captain Biggle. Hank Gratt. All dead. You're telling me they were murdered by Quinn Spain because of me."

Her voice was rising now. "Worse than that," she went on, "You're saying that Uncle Paul Chalfant is in this with him!"

Zack looked at her grimly. "Up to his chin. Up to his black mind."

She broke then. She began to shake. "I'll never believe that. Never. He's my mother's brother. My own flesh and blood. Why, he's been like a father to me. I hardly even knew my real father. It was always Uncle Paul. He's always been so kind, so gentle. He could never do such a thing. Never! Never! Never!"

Zack said nothing. It was some time before she could speak calmly again. "I see what you meant when you decided that living with the Crows would be best. What if you can't find this Crow village? What if this man, Belzey Williams, isn't there? What if the Crows are unfriendly?"

She had bowed to his decision, even though she still believed he was wrong and that he had motives in regard to his own safety in refusing to take her to Fort Jeanne.

"We'll jump that hurdle when we reach it," he said.

"How soon can we start?"

"Within a week," he said. "Maybe in

three, four days if you will take it easy and don't bring on a setback."

"All right," she said wearily. "A week. I'll wait."

But the decision had already been made for them, and they had no voice in it. They fell silent as the waning day faded off into chill dusk, and that in turn gave way to wintry darkness.

Jeanne huddled on the pallet, and Zack sat by the fire, long legs folded beneath him. In that moment there was an Indian-like stolidity in him, an acceptance of circumstances and a refusal to anticipate the future.

She watched him, marking the gauntness of his jaw, the way his belt pinched into his middle. He had tried to hone the knife that day to razor edge in order to shave away the bristle of beard that gave him a raffish appearance. He had spent a long time at it. Even though the effect was patchy and the process painful she could see that he felt more presentable. She had previously noted in him this desire for neatness and his uneasiness at disorder. She watched his hand go absently to the tobacco pouch which he still carried slung around his neck. A little, wry twinge of disappointment crossed his features when he remembered that the pouch was empty. He pulled out the stone pipe, handling it affectionately. He drew on the cold and profitless stem for a time, blew through it, and tucked the pipe once again back in the pouch. She had seen him go through this routine many times.

Sera was carefully washing the makeshift items which Zack had whittled to serve as dishes and eating utensils. The copper kettle was the treasure among these, and Sera handled it as loving as Zack treated his pipe.

The dark shadow of the mystery of Paul Chalfant and Quinn Spain lay over them, but at least a definite decision had been made as to their destination after their departure from this lonely place. All of them were more content now that they had an objective to think about.

However, Zack's thoughts were not on Chalfant or Quinn Spain but continued to linger on his empty tobacco pouch. He missed his smoking. He was mentally anticipating the enjoyment of his pipe once again some day. Or a good cigar. Or of sipping a drink of mulled, spiced rum. He recalled a cold, rainy day when he sat in a tavern in the *Vide Poche*, or empty pocket, as the gay section of St. Louis was called, amid convivial companions, with a steaming tankard in his hand, watching a creole wench dance to the music of a zither and show her stockings. That led to memories of another day — this time a day of sweat and July heat on a keelboat with his brother when he had come aboard after helping on the cordelle, and bottles of porter, chilled in a cold-water spring that had been found at riverside, were handed to him and to the other men. He could recall its musty tang.

These were pleasant memories. He was smiling a little, and Jeanne found herself miffed that she was not sharing his thoughts. She took it for granted that the reveries of a man who had led a life such as his must be taking him through Homeric scenes and violent days.

Zack's head lifted suddenly and he was back in this bleak camp with the glow of the fire marking out the sudden alertness in his face.

He knew that Jeanne had seen this, and he lifted a warning hand before she could speak, silencing her.

He heard it again. The faintest whisking sound of a foot or a knee sliding across rock.

Someone was out there on the knob!

Sparks were rising from the fire, sweeping above the rim of the hideout, generated from some popping segment of dry brush which Sera had been feeding the flames. Days of security had made them careless, and none of them had noticed this betrayal of their sanctuary.

Zack came to his feet in a lunging thrust of movement. As he did so the figure of a man arose into view above him.

The intruder was Jules Lebow, the massive member of Quinn Spain's aides, and the man who had used the whip on Zack.

Lebow held a rifle, and it was trained on Zack, point-blank. Zack, helped by the momentum of his rising, plunged ahead beneath the gun and batted it upward as it was fired, sending the bullet wild.

Lebow tried to retreat but Zack leaped, grasping his ankle. The man lifted the rifle, bringing its muzzle chopping savagely down in an attempt to brain. Zack jerked the man off his feet and dragged him into the niche with him, defeating that attempt.

They fell together, Lebow on top. He was kicking and clawing but he had lost the rifle in the fall. One hand was seeking the handle of a knife that was scabbarded on a wide leather belt that he wore outside his fur-trimmed Fitzhugh Fur capote.

He managed to draw the knife in spite of Zack's efforts. He had Zack at a disadvantage and would have driven the blade home, but Sera leaped in and caught his arm, sending the weight of her body against him. That overbalanced him, and Zack came to his knees on even terms.

Sera was whirled aside by their violence as they twisted, slugging, gouging, and butting. They stumbled over her body and went down.

Jeanne leaped from her blankets and seized up the Indian rifle Zack had brought to the sanctuary and stood waiting a chance to fire, but feared to do so, so violent was the combat.

Zack's own knife lay on a flat rock by the fire. He rolled to it, snatched it up and came to his feet. Lebow was coming at him, and he lifted the knife and drew it up in a slashing movement.

Lebow impaled himself on the blade because of his own weight and ferocity. He struck weakly with his knife but it barely grazed Zack's shirt.

Lebow moaned. He weakened, crumpled to his knees and then to the ground, carrying Zack with him. His life's blood was gushing into the earth.

Zack got to his feet. He could not speak

for a time, so utterly had his strength been drained in those seconds of battle. He took the rifle from Jeanne's hands and stood crouched, gazing tensely at the rim of the crevice.

He was taking it for granted that there were more of them out there. It did not seem possible that Lebow could have been alone. But the seconds passed, and there was only the rasp of his own breathing and the gasping of Lebow who was quivering in the final spasm of death at his feet.

Zack finally moved slowly, cautiously, and peered over the rim of the Owl's Nest. Only the blackness of the wintry night met his eyes. Wan stars showed through a misty overcast.

Foes might be crouching on the ledges below the knob. He listened but could hear nothing. There was no wind at the moment to conceal sounds.

He pulled himself to the surface and descended. Circling cautiously he became convinced that there were no other opponents on the bluff.

The wailing, lost-baby cry of a bobcat drifted from a distance in the darkness below. The call came again, rising from another point.

Zack returned to the sanctuary and

kicked dirt on the fire, deadening it to a faint glow so that no spark would rise. Lebow's body lay twisted partly on its side.

"He wasn't alone," Zack said. "There are others out there. They're signaling. They must have heard the shot, but I don't believe they know from which direction it came."

He was silent a moment, thinking. "I wasn't as slick at fooling them as I thought," he said.

"They must have tracked you here after all," Jeanne said.

Zack shook his head. "More likely they got around to adding two and two together and made a good guess."

"I see what you mean," she said. "You stole a gun and food at the Mandan town. You also took the clothes from the Indian woman and other clothes and blankets. That told them there was more than one of you and that at least one was a woman. They guessed that whoever that person was she could not have traveled far from where the keelboat was ambushed."

Zack nodded. "The weather was against them until now, but they finally came back to this place to look around. I doubt if there were more than three or four of them. White men and not Indians, probably. They likely separated and spread out during the day to look for tracks. That's why Lebow was alone. They may have a camp near. Maybe they thought that shot was a signal from Lebow, asking them to lead him in to where they are."

He paused, then added: "They'll know before long that something's happened to Lebow, and will begin looking around. They might search the bluff. We've got to pull out. At once."

"At once?" Sera echoed aghast. "But . . . !"

Zack eyed Jeanne wryly. "I said I'd be hanged if I wanted to carry you on my back all the way to the Little Buffalo. It looks like I didn't know what I was talking about."

"You can't do it, of course," she said. "After all, I'm a little scrawny right now, but I'm still a full-grown person. Let's face facts."

"And these facts?"

"I will keep going as long as I'm not a danger to you and Sera," she said. "When I decide that I am, you two will go on. I'll join you later."

"Bosh!" Sera snorted. "Let's not be dramatic. I won't listen to such nonsense."

"No harm in listening," Zack said.

That silenced Sera. She stared, incredulous and horrified, as Zack calmly began preparations. "Wear everything you can," he said. He looked at Jeanne and added, "Stick to men's breeches. It'll make it handier if I have to lug you along."

Zack was especially particular about their footwear. The brogans and moccasins that he had gathered were a treasure, and he spent precious time binding and rebinding the feet of the two women with strips of cloth and fitting and refitting them.

Sera had insisted on staying with skirts, saying that she wouldn't be caught dead in men's clothes. She now gazed dolefully down at the result after Zack had given grudging approval to her costume. "I might have looked at things different if I'd had your figure, Jeanne," she sighed. "I wouldn't want to be caught dead in this costume either."

Zack formed the blankets into ponchos, by cutting openings for their heads. Sera carried their meager supply of food and what few spare items of apparel they had, along with the bow and quiver of arrows. Zack slung the rifles across his chest, along with the ammunition and hatchet and copper kettle.

He appraised Jeanne. "That'll help balance me," he mused. "I'd say you're down to around a hundred pounds. Maybe three or four above that, now that you're starting to fatten again. It will have to be pick-a-back."

He covered the body of Jules Lebow with loose rocks as best he could as a protection against animals. He scattered the embers of the fire and kicked earth over them.

"This place fooled them before," he said. "It might never be found by Lebow's friends. But they'll figure that whoever raided the Mandan village had something to do with him turning up missing. At best, all we can expect is a day or two leeway before they quit looking for him and begin hunting our trail again. Maybe it will snow again. If so, even if they find the Owl's Nest they might not see anything that will tell them anything for sure."

They stood for a moment in the darkness. Now that the fire was out, this place was no longer a sanctuary but a tomb, Zack felt dead in mind.

He wondered if any of them would live to reach the Little Buffalo. He had told the women that the stream was beyond the breaks in the plains to the south, but the fact was that he was only guessing. He was not familiar with the terrain and he had no way of knowing how far south of the breaks the stream might lie. Or they might never find it.

There was one factor he had not mentioned. Their route would be southwesterly rather than south. The Missouri also veered south beyond this area, so that their journey would actually bring them nearer Fort Jeanne than they now were by perhaps a score of miles.

Even if they did find the Crow village there was a question which Jeanne had brought up previously that he could not answer. He had no way of knowing if the Crows would take them in or kill them. The Crows were an unpredictable people. If Belzey Williams was living with them with his two wives, the odds might be in their favor, but Belzey was as nomadic and changeable of mind as the Indians. He could have shifted his plans and wintered elsewhere.

"We'll follow frozen ground as much as possible," he said. "It's my opinion that away from the river is the one direction they figure we won't go. They're only open plains in that point of the compass. They'll expect us to head upstream and try to make it to the fort or follow the river down to get out of the country."

He helped Sera scramble out of the Owl's Nest. He lifted Jeanne bodily to the surface, tossed the packs, and joined them. Jeanne stood erect. She was breathing fast.

A wind as harsh as broken glass drove at them. The women moved closer together. He knew how they felt, for he had the same sensation. Naked, exposed, torn from the shelter that had been a shield so long they had come to depend upon it.

He adjusted his equipment, shrugging it into tolerably comfortable positions, and looked at Jeanne. "All right," he said.

She hesitated, then placed her arms around his shoulders, and he lifted her on his back.

"No more talk," he said.

He picked his way down the bluff, giving a hand to Sera at times. Reaching the brush where he had encountered the elk, they worked their way to the flood bank and mounted to the open plain. He halted often to listen, but there was no indication that any danger was near.

He estimated that the breaks in the plain must be ten miles or more to the southwest. This offered the first chance of real concealment. When daylight came, anything that moved on the open expanse of country would no doubt be sighted by anyone watching from vantage points. By daybreak they must be off these snow-dappled flats if they hoped to escape immediate pursuit.

"Let me walk for a while," Jeanne said.

He set her down, and she moved along with him, a hand on his arm. She kept it up for ten minutes. She began to lag, and he carried her again.

"You were right," she sighed. "A week's time would have been better."

Zack moved steadily with his burden. The cold wind was a following wind, and that helped them along. He feared that a new storm was in the making. It might shield them. It might also kill them if it caught them without shelter.

CHAPTER TWELVE

During the first miles Zack rested only at long intervals. Sera, showing determined endurance, kept pace. Jeanne insisted on walking for such short distances as her strength permitted. A new sickle moon was low in the sky, giving some light to guide their way over the hummocky plain.

Soon the moon went down. The wind blew colder and the under-footing seemed to grow more treacherous. They tripped with maddening regularity over tough roots of sagebrush and at times stumbled into shallow gullies that were not visible in the darkness.

Zack was tiring, and so was Sera. Midnight came, according to the swinging of the stars, and he had no way of knowing the extent of their progress. Their universe was the dim plain stretching endlessly around them in the starlight.

Zack stumbled again and went to his knees. This time Jeanne pushed him away when he attempted to rise and carry her again.

"It was agreed that you two will go on

and I will follow," she said.

"There was no agreement," Zack said savagely.

He slung the pack on his back and lifted her almost forcibly in his arms, carrying her thus. The clash seemed to give him angry strength, and he kept going. Dawn showed at last. The gray pallor that lightened the sky seemed reluctant to reach the frozen earth. Blackness still lay ahead. Suddenly he realized that this blackness was the heavy bulk of hills and flat-topped bluffs. They were near the rough country.

He had been close to the end of his tether. The intervals during which he had been forced to halt with his burden and rest had grown in frequency as the night had advanced. Jeanne had insisted often on walking, but these attempts also had grown shorter and shorter before her strength failed. Sera also was equally weary.

Revived by the knowledge that shelter was near, they hurried almost at a run. Soon they stumbled down the banks of a ravine where a partly frozen creek glinted among bare willows. They had made it off the open flats in time. They now had a covert and the means for a fire. Presently they were all asleep.

Zack awakened twice during the morning and left the camp silently to climb from the ravine and ascend a bluff from which he could survey their back trail northward. Each time the result was the same. The weather still had not made up its mind, although the day remained overcast. Beneath that gray background, refraction of light created illusions. A small outcrop of boulders nearby was magnified into sizable bluffs. A pair of gray wolves, loping across a snow-covered flat, seemed to be moving among the clouds. The light changed, and they were gone. The Owl's Nest itself loomed up so clearly that it appeared to be close at hand. In the next moment it had faded entirely from vision. The cold, wind-whipped plain lay vacant. Nothing moved upon it, not even the wolves.

Zack returned each time to camp satisfied there was no immediate pursuit at least. He repeated the trip to the bluff at noon with the same result. When he came back Jeanne and Sera were still asleep, huddled together under the same blankets beside the small fire.

Zack reluctantly awakened them. "We'll have to move on," he said. "We'll travel by daylight the rest of the afternoon."

They resumed the flight. They followed

the creek downstream. Zack was certain that it was a tributary to the Little Buffalo and he began to believe that the main stream might be even nearer than he had hoped.

They surprised a band of deer in a flat and Zack downed a young doe at long range. They ate venison beside their campfire. That and a full night's sleep helped them all, especially Jeanne. She walked, clinging to Zack's arm, when they set out in the morning, until Sera insisted that she let Zack carry her.

Zack discovered that the stream was being trapped. He pointed. "See the bent willows? They mark traps. That's a white man's way of setting."

"Beaver?" Jeanne asked.

"Mink, muskrat, and marten," Zack said. "There are beaver here but their fur won't come prime until spring when they come out of their houses and begin working in cold water. Pelts on the smaller stuff are prime now. That's nature's way."

Later on he studied a moccasin track which was very plain at the stream's margin. "That's a white man's foot," he said. "About Belzey Williams's size, I'd say. This might be his trap line. Somebody will be along, running it, sooner or later. We'll hole up and wait."

They camped in a draw from which Zack could keep the creek under observation. It was past noon the next day when he spotted a lank figure, wrapped in a blanket, moving along the creek, a catch bag on his back in which he was carrying the game his trap line had produced.

Zack walked into sight, grinning. "Belzey, you old yoo-haw! Lucky I'm not a Blackfoot, or you'd be shy your hair."

Belzey Williams snatched for his rifle which was slung across his shoulders. He lowered the gun and peered. "I tell yuh, now," he complained in his high, thin voice. "You give me a skeer, an' that's a fact. I'm gittin' mighty careless."

Belzey stared as Jeanne and Sera appeared. "Now, you do stun a man," he said. "This hoss has been through odd doin's in his day, but I never yit seen two purty females come out'n the brush dressed jist like thet. Air they supposed to be squaws?"

"Not yet, but we're well on the way," Jeanne said.

Belzey had carried out his intention of wintering with his wives' people. The Crow village was some ten miles away, where the creek joined the Little Buffalo.

" 'Taint much of a village," Belzey explained. "But thet's all the more reason they'll be glad to have another hunter to help fetch meat. A'ter they git a look at the size o' you, there won't be any complaints, you hear me now. You even top Owl by an' inch, I'd say. An' he's a purty nice-sized Crow."

"Owl?" Zack questioned.

"He's the chief," Belzey said.

Zack looked at Jeanne and Sera. "The owl must be our good-medicine sign," he said. "Maybe we've found another Owl's Nest."

"They'll be still more happy to have you aroun' if them cussed Rees come back," Belzey added.

"Rees?"

"Bunch of 'em hit us just before the first snow an' run off half the ponies," Belzey said. "They might take it into their minds to try ag'in."

Snow touched Zack's face. Feather flakes were drifting in the wind. He looked at the two women. "We're joining the Crows," he said.

Jeanne said nothing, but he could see that she was not reconciled to this.

Zack helped Belzey reset his traps. They fled down the creek before the increasing storm. The temperature was plunging so that the scant snow squealed beneath their feet. The wind began to drive the snow with it. The pellets were grainy hard and stung the skin.

Zack carried Jeanne. Belzey attempted to help Sera, but she would have none of that. "You're the one who's living in sin with two wives, aren't you?" she sniffed. "I'd prefer that you keep your distance."

"Sin, ma'am?" Belzey snorted. "I've heerd no complaints from the interested parties."

They emerged at last into view of the Little Buffalo. The frozen river, dim through the storm, stretched flat and bleak across the face of the open plains.

Near at hand, unutterably lonely in aspect, a score of lodges were huddled in the lee of a low, rocky rise. This was the Crow village.

Zack saw the dread in Jeanne and Sera, the desolation of their minds. "You're wrong," he said. "Wait."

Belzey ran ahead to pave the way for them and returned, beckoning and nodding cheerfully. As they entered the village brown faces gazed out at them from the wind-whipped lodges. But only with curiosity, not hostility.

Belzey led them to his lodge and held the flap open for them to enter. Warmth — blood-stirring warmth — enfolded them as they stepped in.

Belzey was an expert hunter, and his two wives had given him a home that was far above average. Beavertail was simmering in the pot. The smoke wings were adjusted so that the interior was enjoying a maximum of benefit from the fire and a minimum of discomfort from the smoke despite the gusty storm.

Buffalo robes and other game pelts softened the floor. Sleeping pallets stood close to the walls of the conical lodge. These walls were the hue and texture of parchment. They were made of buffalo leather which had been scraped thin enough to admit a mellow glow of daylight. The wind beat at the lodge. The structure was filled with the whispering and muttering of its resistance, but it would take much violence to bring it down.

Sera spoke in a hushed voice. "It's so warm! So warm! I can't believe it!"

It came to Zack that these two had not been really warm since the loss of the keelboat.

"These here," Belzey said awkwardly, "air Yellow Blossom an' Hunts-The-Rainbow."

Belzey's two wives were present but so shy they had remained sitting cross-legged in the background where they were carrying on one of the endless tasks of Indian women. In this case it was moccasin-making. Yellow Blossom was joining the sole to the upper, an operation which apparently could be accomplished satisfactorily only by vigorous use of the teeth and diligent chewing to weld the buckskin. This she was doing.

Hunts-The-Rainbow's shyness was feigned. She was with child and was therefore being pampered. Aware of her superior position, she was gazing down her nose a trifle at these white, unmarried females. She said something to Yellow Blossom in the Crow language that was, obviously, not complimentary.

Belzey became fumingly annoyed. "Thet's no ways to be neighborly, you bad woman," he raged. "Fer a feather I'd take a lodgepole to you."

He said apologetically to Jeanne and Sera: "Two of 'em air just twice as sassy as one wife. Sometimes I'm mighty happy to be out on my trap line."

Sera uttered only a sniff and tilted her chin a trifle higher.

Jeanne walked around the fire to where

the two Indian women sat. She gazed admiringly at their handiwork. "How nice," she said. "How neatly you work. Perhaps some day you'll teach me."

Belzey translated her words. Yellow Blossom and Hunts-The-Rainbow covered their mouths with their hands, for it is very improper for one to reveal startled laughter to a stranger. Hunts-The-Rainbow presently darted a shy look at Jeanne and nodded. She giggled and hid her face.

"They'll git along," Belzey predicted. "Looks like yore tow headed gal is cut from the same strip o' whang leather as them Crow women, Zack. Needs considerable fattenin' though."

"Well, I never!" Sera said, ruffling like a pouter pigeon.

"An' you too, ma'am," Belzey said. "You're a right nice figger of a woman, now thet I git a good look at you."

Sera blanched and backed hurriedly away. Jeanne said, sober-faced, "I believe he's thinking of taking a third wife, Aunt, dear. You may have a proposal in the making."

"Why, you old reprobate!" Sera exploded, giving Belzey a withering glare. "I should think that two wives would be enough to tame you down."

"There's wilder ones than me, you hear me now," Belzey declared, injured. "You just look around, ma'am. You'll find thet I wouldn't be such a poor husband to have."

Sera clapped her hands to her forehead. "The brass of the man!" she moaned. "Why, you lecherous, bigamous old scoundrel, I'd scratch out your eyes if you ever attempted to get gay with me."

Belzey eyed her with growing admiration. "Now there's a gal with spunk," he said. "The kind a man needs to set up his lodge, an' that's a fact."

Sera retreated, taking refuge back of Zack. "Merciful heavens!" she breathed. "Whatever can I do?"

CHAPTER THIRTEEN

Zack rode into the Crow village mounted on a shaggy Indian pony whose coat was matted with frozen snow and icicles. Streamers of frost hung in the air, drifting among the lodges. The smoke from the wings sagged down, floating just above the snow-covered ground as though unable to rise against the weight of the numbing cold.

He was one of nearly a dozen riders, all stiff as sticks from the cold. Yet they were elated. His companions were Crows of the village and they were returning from a week-long hunt, a venture that had taken them into the high plains far to the south.

The pack animals that plodded along with them were heavily laden with buffalo meat. Succulent fleece and hump ribs, great haunches and forequarters. Tongue that could be smoked. Liver and brains and entrails and other delicacies that are dear to the Indian appetite.

Even the personal horses were laden. The hunters themselves had made the return trip mainly on foot to spare the animals, but this was a triumphal entry, and so they came into the village mounted, just as men who had provided meat for the tribe had returned from the good hunts down through the ages.

Zack's mount carried an additional item. Atop the results of the hunt rode a small pine tree. It was little more than three feet high and Zack had carried it many miles, for it was the only one of its kind he had seen in days.

The Crows came pouring from the lodges to greet them. Snow was piled deep around the camp. Drifts in the background rose as high as the tips of the poles, but the core of the community was leveled and blackened by use. The lodges were barricaded with frozen snow, and bore second coverings of buffalo and deer skins over layers of moss and leaves and dry grass as insulation against the cold.

Jeanne appeared, drawing on a wolfskin smock and arranging a fur cowl over her head. Sera gazed briefly from the door of the lodge. She held a bone awl in her hand, being busy, helping Yellow Blossom manufacture a pair of tough high-laced moccasins for Zack's use.

Zack tried to dismount but found that his cold-brittle legs would not respond. Jeanne came hurrying. He used her as a

243

crutch, but she was forced to pull him from the saddle. He clumped woodenly to the ground. Both of them fell, despite her efforts to steady him. She arose and helped him to his feet. They stood laughing.

The drums began sounding triumphantly. The Crow women started a chant of victory. They had been on starvation rations lately and now they would eat their fill once again.

Owl, the stalwart chief, pointed at Zack. "This is the one who brought the luck. He is the one who found the buffalo."

Zack carried the small tree into Belzey's lodge. He was grinning. He said, "Look! It's already decorated. What a shame to let all that pretty foofaraw melt."

Jeanne had followed him. "It can't be!" she cried.

"But it is," Zack said. "It's Christmas Eve. Belzey keeps a calendar, for he traps by the phases of the moon. I checked on dates before we left on the hunt."

She stood gazing at the tree, a variety of emotions playing across her face. He saw loneliness, and that he could understand. Regret, for which there could be many explanations, was there also. But, above all, was gratitude and even an inner contentment. Living with the Crows, she had also learned to live at peace with herself for the time being, at least.

Her hair hung in a braid down her back in the Indian fashion. She had taken to wearing moccasins. She was still thin, for the village had been on short rations lately. Snow glare had tanned her skin.

The women swiftly cooked a meal. After the hunger of all was appeased, Jeanne and Sera lovingly set up the tree. Yellow Blossom and Hunts-The-Rainbow stood by, beaming but mystified. The wintry ornamentation had melted in the warmth of the lodge. Jeanne snipped bits of bright scarlet cloth from remnants in the sewing bags and tied them on the branches. Sera hung a glass bead in the foliage and added a polished bear claw and several elk teeth from a collection that Yellow Blossom was gathering for adorning a ceremonial costume.

The two Indian women, seeing what was wanted, hurried about, finding offerings to add to the yule tree. Other Crows, who had been peering into the lodge, caught the spirit. The village was ransacked. Bits of broken mirror and ornaments of buffalo horn were added to the decorations. Colorful feathers, brass rings, and tinkling hawk's bells were brought in.

One withered old warrior, scarred by

battle and the sun dance, offered a treasured scalp, a memento of some mighty feat of the past. This, Zack managed to assure him diplomatically, should remain always in his own possession.

The little tree was weighed down with the glitter. "It is their big medicine," a Crow father explained to his young son . . . "It is where their gods live."

Tears rolled down Jeanne's face. "I'm glad you remembered," she said to Zack. "I'm ashamed that I did not."

Time had indeed raced by. They had been in the Crow village for weeks. Zack had been taken into the lodge of Owl, while the two white women had remained quartered in Belzey's domicile.

Sera had balked at that arrangement at first. "Imagine living in the same place with a bigamist," she had moaned. "It's a disgrace, that's what it is."

But only a few days in the past Zack had heard her say, with a weary sigh to Hunts-The-Rainbow, "It's a blessing there are two of you. There's no end to the moccasins a man wears out or the buckskins he tears to pieces or the hides that are to be scraped and stretched, and the wood and water that has to be brought in. I only pray for you that the child you're expecting will be a daughter so that she will be some help to you, rather than another of these lazy males who do nothing but sit around and brag about the buffalo they nearly brought down."

Jeanne had entered into the Crow way of life with a facility that surprised Zack. Her recovery had been swift and complete. She worked with the other women, carrying her share of wood and water each morning. Along with Belzey's wives she flensed pelts from game that was brought in, and stretched and scraped the hides on the frames, a task that tried the patience and endurance. She could carve and cook buffalo and elk meat and venison and was learning the art of making garments and moccasins out of the skins. She had picked up the Crow language swiftly.

Yellow Blossom and Hunts-The-Rainbow had formed a bond of affection with her. They treated her as they would a sister. To them, Sera, who had entered the life with a superior attitude that had soon melted, was a wise and sometimes scolding maternal influence to whom they could turn in time of mental stress. Hunts-The-Rainbow's time was at hand, and this was to be a first child. She was young and frightened and was finding great comfort in Sera's presence.

The winter that gripped the plains had been as violent as any in the memory of the old men. Blizzard after blizzard had held them trapped in the lodges for days at a time with only the warmth of the fires offering hope of survival. Between these storms, raw chinooks had visited the plains. These had been almost as hard to bear as the blizzards. They had changed the land into a morass of mud, impassable to men or horses. Then the freezes would come, leaving the terrain mailed in ice.

Only lately had the weather settled. Clear, cold winter prevailed. The plains were hard-frozen, and movement by hunters was possible.

Rations had been short for weeks, for the Crows, in the way of Indians, had lived fat during the summer on the buffalo which had seemed as countless as the clumps of grass on which the herds fed. The store of meat and jerky had been squandered in feasting during the dreamy months of fall, for surely, with the buffalo near at hand by the thousands, there had been no reason for frugality.

The storms had scattered the buffalo. For weeks none had been seen during such times as Zack and the others had been able to hunt. The larder had been almost bare for the past several days. No member of the village, except the very small children, had eaten more than a few scraps in more than forty-eight hours. Jeanne and Sera had once again come to know the meaning and the terror of real famine.

They had also learned the bitter sweetness of sacrifice. They had given their food to the young when their own craving was almost unbearable. At this moment, thinned by fasting, they were reaping the rewards of their hardiness. Knowing that the ordeal was over for the time at least, their thanksgiving and feasting now could be unblemished and without regret.

Zack watched Jeanne as she moved about. The bulky, very practical Crow garb could not entirely disguise the good lines of her figure. With her tawny hair and smoky blue eyes, she could never be mistaken for an Indian woman.

Her gaze came to him as she grew aware of his attention. She attempted no show of false modesty but stood meeting his gray eyes soberly, ready to heed whatever he had to say to her.

He was possessed by a great rush of desire. He was aware that she saw this in him. She straightened a trifle, but did not waver.

She awaited whatever was his decision. This, at least, was Indianlike.

The thought came to him that this readiness, this compliance to his will, was only because she believed he had saved her life. An anger came up in him. He wanted nothing of that sort of reward.

Also Indianlike had been her silence on the subject of Fort Jeanne. During the first days of their presence in the Crow village he had known that each morning she had hoped they would start for the fort. But, as time had passed, and he had not mentioned the matter, she had resigned herself to waiting.

Zack, at first, had feared that she might attempt to make the journey alone, to prove that he was wrong in regard to Paul Chalfant. But she had remained obedient to his unspoken wish.

He wheeled abruptly and left the lodge. He strode to Owl's lodge, which was his own quarters. The village throbbed with activity. Squaws were caring for the buffalo meat which was being divided under Owl's direction. The drums were still sounding, and the Crows, men, women, and children, were gulping at raw liver which they dipped in gall as a condiment. They were partaking of this tidbit while the greater feast of meat was cooking. The eating would continue on through the night and into the dawn no doubt. Christmas dawn.

Belzey followed Zack into the chief's lodge and sank down in his customary position of folded legs. Zack stripped to the skin, ridding himself thankfully of the saddle-stiffened buckskins. Owl's wife, Floating Leaf, who was a large, tall woman, graying at the temples, brought an iron kettle of hot water. She cooled it with snow until it was bearable, then poured it over his shoulders and body.

The water, still stingingly hot, drove some of the weariness from him. He reveled in its warmth until he glowed. The memories of the long miles and the freezing nights in the hunting camps became only that — memories, and no longer a part of the present. He shaved his jaws clean, using Belzey's razor.

Belzey finally removed the pipe from between his teeth and spoke. "Two strangers was here while you was away makin' meat."

Zack paused abruptly in the act of donning a new hunting shirt of yellow-dyed elkskin which Floating Leaf held for him. "Strangers?" he asked slowly. "You mean — white men?"

"Burned woods they was. *Boisbrûlés.* Had gee-gaws fer trade. Hawk's bells, beads, an' such truck. Allowed thet they was free traders. Came on snowshoes. Said the Rees down on Grand River had stole their ponies."

"What did they look like?"

"I didn't see 'em myself. I was away, runnin' my trap line. Old Gray Elk — he's the one what tried to hang a scalp on the Christmas tree tonight — was here. He told me they was Fitzhugh men. He said he had seen both of 'em hangin' around Fort Jeanne in the fall when he went there to trade."

"When were they here?"

"Five days ago."

"Did they come from Fort Jeanne?"

"Come from the south," Belzey said. "Headed out the same way. But that was only a blind. I sent out a couple of young Crows to pick trail an' they brought back word that these *Boisbrûlés* had swung north toward the Missouri. But anyway, they had been holed up in an Indian village before they showed up here."

"How do you know that?"

"It was Gray Elk that knowed it. His nose told him so. Said the burned woods had been livin' long enough among Indians so that they was beginnin' to smell like it.

Fact is, he said they smelled like Mandans. Now I've never been able to scent Indians quite that good, but I've seen other Indians do it."

"Mandans!"

They gazed at each other. Zack had told Belzey the story of the keelboat massacre and of the events that had followed, including his encounter with Quinn Spain in the Mandan house.

"I'm beginning to get a glimmer of what this is all about," Zack said.

"If nothin' else, it means that we better git ready fer trouble, I tell you now," Belzey snorted. "Big trouble."

"We better put out scouts in a hurry," Zack said.

"Already done it," Belzey said. "I've got three young Crows scoutin' north of us. One is Owl's son. They'll warn us."

"Did they see the two white women?" Zack asked.

"I put the same question to Gray Elk. He was certain sure they saw the young Fitzhugh gal. He said she came into camp with the squaws, carryin' wood, while they was here."

"What did they do?"

"Nothin'. Didn't act like they noticed her."

"Did she see them?"

"Reckon so. Gray Elk said she didn't show any interest. Maybe she mistook 'em for Indians. Ain't much difference unless you're used to *Boisbrûlés,* 'specially in winter with everybody bundled up like fat turkeys."

Zack stood frowning. Floating Leaf knelt to draw new moccasins on his feet. He tried to lift her to her own feet. "No," he said in her language. "You are no slave, mother. I will do that."

"It is for the good of all that women use their little strength to save the greater strength of the hunters," she said.

Zack's thoughts went back to the night in the Owl's Nest when Sera had helped him out of his shoes after the futile buffalo hunt. "Of course," he said, and let Floating Leaf go through with a task that she did not consider menial but eminently practical.

"Why would they risk sending scouts into the village?" he ruminated. "They might have known it might warn us."

Belzey drew on his pipe for a moment. "There ain't much here worth takin', except maybe a few scalps," he said. "Anyone could have seen there'd been hard doin's here, an' that we'd been eatin' poor bull an' mighty little o' that. Not even many ponies since the Rees was here. If anybody was goin' to the trouble of hittin' us in the dead o' winter there must be somethin' they was after mighty bad, an' they wanted to make sure it was here."

"And the chances are they found, it," Zack said.

Belzey nodded. "We ain't too strong, if it comes to standin' off a big war party."

Zack considered it. There was, of course, the chance that the pair of visitors had been genuine free traders. On the other hand, their appearance in midwinter was out of the ordinary. All the other evidence was against them.

Zack became certain that Quinn Spain had located them. During the weeks that had passed he had begun to believe that Spain had given them up as dead or out of his reach.

"The last thing I wanted was to cause trouble for the Crows," he said. "I never intended to stay this long, but the weather pinned us down until lately. I had made up my mind to pull out in a day or two. Now, it may be too late."

"Where would you have gone?" Belzey asked. "Fort Jeanne?"

"Jeanne Fitzhugh would want to go

there," Zack said. "In spite of everything she thinks I'm mistaken about Quinn Spain. And, above all, about her uncle. She seems to be sure this Paul Chalfant could do no wrong. You'd think he was a saint the way she keeps up her faith in him."

"Saints don't pizen preachers, I tell you now," Belzey said.

Zack looked at him sharply. "Poison?"

"Remember that fine big deerhound Angus Macleod owned?"

"The one he called MacDuff? Of course."

"Angus Macleod wasn't the only one who died at Fort Jeanne thet night," Belzey said. "MacDuff went to the happy huntin' ground too. An' in the same room. He always slept alongside his owner's bed, they say. But Quinn Spain didn't seem to want anybody to know about the dog passin' away. He handed its carcass out the window to Jules Lebow, wrapped in a blanket, an' Lebow tuk it away. He liked buried it somewheres. Thet happened before anybody knew the preacher was dead."

"How do you know this?" Zack demanded.

"Gray Elk. It happened at the same time

he was at the fort an' saw those two *Boisbrûlés*. He got it from thet old Pawnee who was travelin' with the preacher. The Pawnee seen 'em do away with the dog."

Zack remembered the fork that had been in Angus Macleod's dead hand. And the missionary's habit of tossing food to his canine companion from his plate.

Horror built up in him. Angus Macleod had fallen dead while eating breakfast, evidently. Quinn Spain had said that he had brought the tray to the room personally. But all food and dishes had been removed before Zack or anyone else had been allowed to enter the room.

"Of course," he said, ashen-lipped. "Of course! Why didn't you tell me this before, Belzey?"

"Jest found it out a day or two ago in talkin' to Gray Elk about the two strangers thet was here."

"Why would they commit a murder like that?" The horror grew in Zack. "Paul Chalfant and Angus Macleod were close friends. Angus said so himself."

"Ain't no way of tellin' what's in another man's mind," Belzey said. "Or in his heart."

Floating Leaf handed Zack a fine new jacket of heavy wolfskin. She explained

257

that it was a gift from Belzey's lodge, meaning that it had been made by Jeanne and Sera and the two Crow women.

She held a small mirror for Zack in which to admire himself. "Much damn big pretty," Floating Leaf said in English.

Zack patted her on the shoulder. "May you have many warrior sons, good one," he said, leaving her giggling and pleased, for her child-bearing days were long past.

Zack and Belzey headed for the latter's lodge. Darkness had come. The stars were glittering cold sparks in an even colder universe.

Zack was glad to step into the warmth and conviviality of the lodge. The fire was burning brightly, and fat buffalo fleece was broiling. Jeanne had contrived a tiny tallow candle which burned on the yule tree.

She curtsied to them. She seemed radiant. She and Sera wore skirts now, and waists of red strouding, which they had contrived partly from the garments Zack had acquired, and partly by barter here in the village. Their hair was done in an attempt at fashionable style. It was evident that Jeanne had put aside all doubts for the moment, and all hardships, and meant to make the most of this interlude.

"You look very distinguished in your holiday attire, sir," she said. "Welcome to the festive board. I regret to say that our wine cellar seems to be inaccessible. The weather, you know. I had planned on champagne before dinner. And some fine old madeira with the principal course, which will be buffalo fleece, *à la americaine,* which means eaten with the fingers. I'm sorry. Or would you have preferred something more spirited?"

"Hot minced rum would be the thing on a night like this," he said. "Served in a tall copper mug by a pretty and willing wench with taffy-colored hair. That's been on my mind for a long time."

"You've mentioned the rum before, but this is the first I've heard about the wench," she said. "You ask too much. The rum you shall have, and hot it will be, and spiced. But the other is unavailable on such short notice."

To Zack's amazement she actually handed him a tin cup steaming with a fragrant beverage. "It is hot rum!" he said incredulously after a sip.

"You can thank Belzey," she beamed. "He's been treasuring a keg of it for just such an occasion."

"Bought it from a Canuck trader last fall," Belzey cackled. "Buried it under my pallet, so old Gray Elk wouldn't find it. He's a regular old rumpot."

Owl and Foating Leaf entered, garbed in ceremonial dress. Other Crows came until the lodge was jammed. Cups of hot rum were passed around.

Belzey unveiled another treasure. This was a small music box which gave forth a tinkling tune when the handle was turned. The Crows clapped hands to their mouths.

Jeanne eyed Zack brazenly and drooped an eyelid in a wink.

Zack sprang to his feet. "May I have the honor of this dance, ma'mselle?" he said, bowing.

"It will be a pleasure," she declared demurely.

Her hand lay dwarfed in his big palm and her other hand rested on his arm. He swung her into the rhythm of the music.

They began it sedately enough, circling slowly in a confined space as the Crows crowded together, trying to make more room for them. Belzey turned the crank of the music box with energy, and Jeanne looked up at Zack challengingly.

He whirled her faster. He began kicking up his heels. She bowed and scraped. "You are not as clumsy as I feared so great a bear of a man would be, m'sieu," she said.

"You have danced with these wenches you talk about, yes?"

"Yes," Zack said. "Now watch this."

He cut a buck and wing. He tripped over the feet of a seated Crow and fell sprawling. The lodge rocked with merriment. Zack arose and swung Jeanne until her feet left the ground. She was breathless with laughter. She screamed for mercy. Finally Zack set her down, and they slumped into their seats, gasping.

"I declare," Sera remonstrated. "I never saw such a display. Showing your ankles like that, young lady. For shame."

Zack and Jeanne sat side by side. The feasting went on and the Crows would not let Belzey quit on the music box.

After a time, as though reluctant to break this mood, Jeanne spoke: "What is it to be?"

He eyed her questioningly. She smiled faintly. "There's been something on your mind, but you didn't want to spoil the fun. I believe I know what it is. Belzey has told you about the two strangers."

"So you did see them?" Zack answered.

"And they saw me. They were careful to act as though they hadn't noticed. But they knew."

That clinched it. If the two visitors had

been wandering traders they would at least have shown curiosity in regard to the presence of a white woman in the Crow village.

He did not want to end this carefree evening. She was waiting for his answer to her original question. It was a harsh decision.

Again he saw something Indianlike in the patience with which she was obedient to his judgment. If anything, the hardships of the past weeks had added to her beauty. Her cheeks were still thin beneath her good cheekbones, and faint shadows remained beneath her eyes, but her experience here, living the full and busy life of a worker of the village, had added depths of maturity that was like an inner flame.

Among the things she had learned, Zack comprehended, was the simplicity of existence, the little that humans really need for contentment — a warm fire, food, a pallet on which to sleep, and companionship. She had seen the way the Crow women existed for the happiness of their men. She had watched the men ride out on the hunt or stand ready to defend the village in battle. Whether this arrangement was fair or not was beyond the question. It was not a compromise with life. It was a way of life.

There could be only one answer to her question, and Zack had arrived at it long before it had been asked. The thing that should be done seemed clear to him, but sitting here amid the music and the feasting, gazing at this comely person at his side, a bitter protest was in him at the necessity that was being forced on him.

Still he went ahead with it. "You and Sera have got to leave."

She seemed to have expected this. "When?" she asked.

"Tomorrow. At daybreak."

"Surely there's no danger that soon?"

"If there's danger at all it will be soon, but there's no telling when. I'll send Belzey with you. And Gray Elk."

"And you?"

"I'll stay here awhile," Zack said.

"And fight alongside the Crows?"

"It might not come to that. Likely we're only painting our own ghosts on the lodge walls."

"Where will we go?" she asked. "To Fort Jeanne?"

"No," Zack said sharply. "There's another Crow village down in the Pumpkin Butte country. A big village where you'll be safe. It will be a hard trip, but you can make it in less than a week."

"Why not Fort Jeanne?"

"I have my reasons," Zack said.

"The only way this terrible thing can be straightened out is by me talking to Uncle Paul," she said. "Surely, you must see that."

"It's best to do it my way," he said.

She did not pursue the subject. Perhaps she feared that down that path lay terrible answers.

Instead, she said, her voice matter-of-fact, "I'll stay here, of course."

"If they come, you might be the one they want to kill above all," Zack said.

"You really believe that, don't you?" she replied. "And I know that you must be wrong. In any event it could not change what I must do. I have to stay. You surely must know that I would."

Zack sat looking at his hands which rested on his knees. They were roughened by winter and the hard usage of the buffalo hunt. She sat in a similar fashion, legs folded. Her hands too, he noted, were reddened and marked by toil.

"Yes," he said. "I knew it."

She nodded. "These people have sheltered us," she said. "They're more than friends. We're one of them. If a fight comes, I'm the cause of it. The least I can do is help them face it."

"Yes," he said. "I know."

She gave him one of her grave inspections. "I'm glad you know," she said.

"Glad?"

"It means you've come to learn more about me. About what I really am, and how I really feel."

She was silent a moment, then said, "I could stay here always. I could be happy here."

If he stayed here with her. He knew that this was what she meant. She was afraid of what she might find if she went to Fort Jeanne, afraid to learn that her own flesh and blood had turned against her and was even trying to murder her. She wanted to hide from all the ugliness of such a reality.

She spoke again, wryly. "But it has to be faced sooner or later. There's been a terrible mistake somewhere. I tell you that I know Uncle Paul too well to believe anything else."

Zack knew there was no mistake. Paul Chalfant must be involved with Spain, not only in looting the company but in the keelboat massacre and the murder of Angus Macleod. The latter crime seemed completely callous. The only motive Zack could ascribe was that Chalfant and Spain must have known that the missionary had come to Fort Jeanne to look into stories he had heard of their chicanery.

They would have wanted no prying into their affairs. Above all, they would not have wanted a voice as powerful as the missionary's raised against them. Another factor was the sables. Angus Macleod would have been the only witness against them if that matter was brought to light. They had believed, no doubt, that Zack, without weapons, would never live through the winter on the plains.

Jeanne was watching him. "You know more than you have told me," she said.

He avoided that bait. "What about Sera?" he asked.

"She will stay also, of course. You couldn't drag her away, especially with Rainbow's baby so near. You'd think that Rainbow was her daughter the way she's been worrying about her."

Owl arose and began a solemn shuffle dance to the lively rhythm of the music box. Other Crows joined in as best they could in the crowded lodge.

Sera's voice finally imperiously put a stop to the merriment. "That's enough. Clear out of here, you drunken men. Scat! Scat! Scat, I say!"

Hunts-The-Rainbow's moment had come. Zack, along with the men, emerged whooping into the bitter starlight. The warriors slapped Belzey on the back, joshing him in Crow and in sign language, both of which were couched in frank terms and gestures.

The expectant father drank the last horn of rum, from brim to tip without pausing. Zack and Owl finally carried him, triumphantly drunk, to Owl's lodge and put him to bed.

The village, the great feast at the white man's medicine tree over, began to quiet down for the night. Zack questioned Owl about the scouts who had been sent north to guard against surprise. The chief assured him that the three young men who were charged with this duty were reliable. One was Owl's own son, Zack was reminded a trifle testily. Owl had great pride in his offspring.

Zack computed the chances, as he prepared to turn in. It had been five days since the mysterious visitors had come to the village. That was time enough for them to have crossed the Missouri to the Mandan towns, and for a war party to be on its way south. It was possible, but he believed it was hardly probable that the Mandans would have moved that swiftly.

Belzey was snoring loudly, and Owl was

asleep also. Floating Leaf had gone to Belzey's lodge to join Sera in looking after Hunts-The-Rainbow.

Zack lay awake. Sounds from Belzey's lodge ran across the silence of the night occasionally. Each time sleep receded farther from him. Motherhood was not being easy for Hunts-The-Rainbow.

It was past midnight when the sounds reached a climax that brought cold sweat to Zack's forehead and a sickness within him.

He sat up suddenly, listening. A thin new wailing ran through the night. The screaming of Hunts-The-Rainbow had ended.

He shook the snoring Belzey. "Wake up! Wake up! You're a father! The baby's here!"

But Belzey only mumbled and rolled over. Zack arose and dressed. He walked to Belzey's lodge. "Is everything all right?" he called, standing outside the entrance.

It was Jeanne who answered. "Come in."

He pushed aside the robe that covered the opening and stepped in. The lodge was steamy hot, for the fire had been kept blazing.

She and Yellow Blossom held a new, small brown squalling object and were washing it. Perspiration glistened on the bronze skin of the Indian women and on Jeanne's white flesh.

Jeanne was smiling. She fondled the infant. Her eyes were swimming. "A son," she said, and she was weeping. "A hunter of the buffalo. A warrior to fight for his people."

Zack walked nearer. He gathered both the child and Jeanne Fitzhugh in his arms. He kissed her savagely, demandingly. Her lips responded steadily, fully to him.

He drew back abruptly. He said harshly, "No! This is not for us."

He drew away. He left her standing there, holding the Indian baby against her bosom. He went back to Owl's lodge where Belzey still lay asleep.

After a time Zack slept also, soundly, soothingly. For a moment, at least, when he had felt her lips respond on his, all had seemed right with the world.

He awakened suddenly. The lodge was as black as midnight, the fire nearly dead. The cold had crept in.

A rider was galloping into the village. He heard Crows awakening in other lodges. Owl came out of his robes and fumbled for his rifle. Belzey still snored.

Zack pulled on moccasins and was the

first one out of the lodge, his rifle capped and ready. Overhead the stars were tarnished. A planet in the east was blazing into great brilliance. Dawn was at hand.

The horseman called out in the Crow tongue as he raced nearer, and rifles were lowered. It was Hawk, the son of Owl.

Hawk shouted his message as he leaped from his pony. "The Mandans! They are coming! They are near!"

Everything was not right with the world after all. Five days had indeed been long enough for a war party to be brought across the frozen Missouri and to the Little Buffalo.

The young Crow rattled out the news. The Mandans had surmised that scouts would be out and had circled well to the east, as though they were heading for the Ree country, but had approached from that direction. Evidently they had left their ponies out on the plains, for they were now on foot in the hope of effecting surprise.

There was no way of knowing their numbers, Hawk said. Their presence had been discovered only by chance. The raiding party was split. One group was moving up the Little Buffalo from the east. The other party had circled to the north and vanished into the breaks of the creek which emptied into the main river just above the village.

"If they're coming at us from two sides," Zack said to Owl, "maybe we can hit 'em one at a time."

CHAPTER FOURTEEN

Christmas morning. Daybreak marked out the frigid bleakness of the plains. The snowbound lodges of the Crows stood silent and apparently asleep as the light strengthened. Thin smoke drifted from the wings. The small, intermittent stirring of a bitter wind tightened the leathery walls of the lodges against the framework of poles, giving the structures a starving, skeletonlike aspect.

The small herd of hobbled ponies came drifting from a gully where they had huddled for warmth during the night. The animals began pawing for forage in the frozen flats along the river.

In the village nothing moved. A sound came from Belzey Williams's lodge. It was the mewing-kitten voice of a newborn baby.

This was the only lodge that was occupied. Hunts-The-Rainbow could not be moved without bringing on certain death. Both Sera and Yellow Blossom had remained with her. Barricades had been built in the lodge to shelter them all in case of need.

Zack crouched in hiding in a depression in the snow a dozen feet back from the rim of the rocky ridge which overlooked the village. The tip of the nearest lodge was no more than a pistol shot away.

Owl was concealed a few yards to his left. Belzey was close beside him to the right, so close they could talk in murmurs. Their position commanded the terrain for a considerable distance and there was little danger that a whisper would reach a foe before he approached within sight.

Dug into the snow or crouching back of brush and boulders along the rim were the Crows. They lay huddled in robes and blankets, waiting in silence. Rifles and bows and what sidearms they possessed were being kept warm by their bodies. Particularly sensitive to the cold were the bows, and although the severe weather of the past few days had moderated somewhat Zack estimated that the temperature was still not far above zero.

War axes, hatchets, and clubs lay in the open, along with quivers of arrows. Some of the warriors had knives, and a few owned lances with metal tips. Zack saw at least two of the old-time ivory daggers, formed from walrus tusks which had come down from the north in trade long in the past and had been handed down through the generations. There were two stone-headed war axes, bound with rawhide. Weapons from another age.

The squaws were present also, hidden back of the line of warriors. They too were armed with clubs and hatchets.

Jeanne was with the women. She had no weapon. She had said only one thing to Zack as he and Owl and Belzey were deploying their forces. "I pray to the Almighty that this can be stopped in time."

Zack had placed a hand under her chin, lifted her head and forced her to look at him. "Listen to me," he had said. "These people have fought the Mandans before. They have fought other tribes. They will fight again. You can no more change this than you could stop the wind from blowing, or spare that girl the suffering that brought a baby into this life. Don't try to carry the world on your shoulders. At least this world."

"This is the only world that matters right now," she had responded. "This one that's right around us. This is all wrong, and I feel that I am the cause."

She had left him, drawing her blanket tighter around her. She was pale, her eyes tragic. Beneath the blanket she wore the deerskin smock, leggings, and heavy petticoats of a squaw. Zack had requested that she dress herself thus. She had asked no questions, but she had known that he had wanted this so that she could not be easily singled out from the Crow women.

Belzey spoke from his place at Zack's elbow. "Waugh! This child's tongue feels as rough as beaver claws. I'm half froze for a drink o' rum."

"You drank the last of it after the party," Zack said. He was silent a moment, then spoke again. "Why would a man like Paul Chalfant stand for the murder of a friend, or be a party to it? Jeanne still has faith in Chalfant. Why would a man change like that?"

"Maybe the preacher was done in before Chalfant had any say about it," Belzey said. "Chalfant was away that night, accordin' to what you told me. Looks like Spain didn't want him to git together with Angus an' talk over old times."

"I've always doubted that Chalfant was really away," Zack said. "I think he was there at the fort all the time, but didn't want to talk to Angus because. . . ."

His voice drifted off. He gazed at Belzey, startled. "That's it!" he exclaimed. "That's it! Why didn't I see this before? It's as plain as —"

He quit talking. One of the Crows who had been posted as lookout, was signaling that the foe was in sight down the river. Owl and Zack wormed to the edge of the bluff and waited.

Presently, in the strengthening daylight, Zack glimpsed the Mandans. They were moving in a ragged line through the thin brush that flanked the frozen surface of the river.

Zack estimated that there were some thirty of them in sight. The other half of the war party would number about the same no doubt, but it had not yet appeared from the mouth of the creek upstream. The Crows would be outnumbered more than two to one.

This was no mere horse-stealing raid. The Mandans had come in force. These doubtlessly were from the town where Zack had encountered Quinn Spain and the larger community he had sighted nearby. These were the Mandans who had ambushed the keelboat.

Instead of waiting for their companions to appear from upriver, the first contingent broke into a run. They had sighted the un-defended Crow lodges and were inflamed by the belief that they had easy prey in sight and a chance to claim all the glory themselves — and all the scalps.

Owl motioned to his Crows, and they came crawling forward to the rim of the bluff, rifles ready and arrows nocked to bowstrings.

Owl arose and lifted a warwhoop. He shouted an insult and gestured derisively. The Mandans gazed up with dark faces and Zack could see the awful consternation in them as they poised there, knowing how exposed they were to the blast that was about to strike them.

It came. Guns exploded. Some were old fusils with flare-mouthed muzzles, loaded with slugs. Others were Kentucky long rifles or Hawken guns. There were muskets, wrapped with rawhide, that had been brought down from Canada by the traders in the early days. And a few good caplocks. They all dealt death and injury, hurling many of the Mandans, bleeding and torn, to the white snow.

It was the bows, their twanging harsh in the brittle air, that were taking the heaviest toll. A third of the Mandans were struck down in the first few seconds. The remainder scattered, frantically seeking cover. The Crow bowstrings continued their dismal chorus and more of their quarry were pinned to the snow by shafts through their bodies.

The Mandans began shooting back, using both rifles and bows, but they had as targets only the heads and shoulders of their opponents on the low ridge.

Zack had not used his rifle. Arrows passed close by as resistance increased, but he withheld his fire. He kept gazing upstream. The second segment of the attacking force had not yet appeared. The warrior the Crows had stationed as a lookout in that direction had abandoned his place and had raced back to join in the slaughter of the hated Mandans.

Battle lust blinded the Crows. Even Owl. Wild with the thought of victory, thirsty to come to grips with their enemy, they poured down from the bluff and swept upon the surviving Indians with knives and clubs in their hands.

Zack arose and shouted in the Crow tongue. "Come back! You are fools!"

If they heard him they did not heed. The thing Zack had feared now happened. More Mandans appeared west of the village. The second half of the raiding party had arrived.

The Crows were fiercely engaged in attempting to wipe out the original force of attackers. They were paying a price for throwing away the advantage they had held. The surviving Mandans, cornered, were fighting fiercely. Crows were falling. Half a dozen separate hand-to-hand melees were going on.

Zack left the bluff and went raging among them, shouting at the Crows, and pointing upstream toward the new Mandan force. Up to this moment the battle had been fought away from the village itself. The first party had been halted just short of that objective, but the new arrivals were already racing among the lodges.

The Crows, fresh scalps in the hands of many, turned to meet this new onslaught.

"Get back on the ridge," Zack kept shouting. "You've got the best of it from there. They're too many for you down here."

He became aware that another voice was lifted, and that Crows around him were slowing a little and gazing.

Jeanne stood in plain sight on the ridge nearby. She had removed the cowl from her head so that all could see her tawny hair and know that she was not an Indian woman.

"No more fighting!" she was shouting. There was a desperate urgency in her that gave her strength and power. Her voice carried. The din of battle tapered off. The bowstrings went silent. The Mandans also were staring.

"No fighting!" she repeated. She spoke partly in Crow and partly in English, and used gestures to get her meaning across. "You can see me, all of you. There has been a terrible mistake. I am J. K. Fitzhugh of the fur company. I am a woman, but the company came into my name when my father died. I am the friend of the Mandans. I am the friend of the Crow. Let us put down your arms and we will talk. . . ."

Zack went scrambling up the bluff. She saw him coming and talked desperately faster. "I will go to Fort Jeanne with your chiefs and there we will meet with the *bourgeois* and . . ."

Zack, reaching the crest of the rise, had a clear view of the Mandan force. They were scattered among the lodges and still moving forward but were holding their fire, still amazed by the appearance of the white girl.

But not all of them. In the background Zack saw a man lift a rifle and take aim. A second did the same. They were muffled in heavy buffalo robes, but beneath these he could see the heavy winter leggings and striped breeches of *voyageurs*.

Zack reached Jeanne in the next instant, seized her, and snatched her flat on the snow. He heard the report of the rifles and the whir of the bullets over the spot where she had been standing.

They lay face to face. She began to weep in a dreadful way. "All those poor dead people!" she sobbed. "I must stop it. I must! I must! Before it is too late."

"Getting yourself killed won't help," Zack said. "There's no stopping it right now."

The battle had resumed with a great burst of screeching and gunfire. Zack left Jeanne huddled there, sobbing, and leaped down the bluff again. The Crows were advancing to defend their lodges, but they were still overwhelmingly outnumbered.

"Get them back on the bluff!" Zack shouted at Owl.

Owl emerged from the frenzy of scalping and became a leader again, a war chief. He shouted orders. The Crows understood and followed him and Zack to cover on the rim of the rise. From that position their arrows and bullets began to take toll.

The Mandans, seeing the scalped bodies of their companions beyond the village, suddenly lost heart. They turned and fled, racing back through the village and toward shelter in the brush of the creek from which they had emerged. A few reckless Crows once again left the bluff and followed them but were trapped and slain and scalped for their boldness.

The last of the Mandans vanished from the river bottom. The yelling and the flight of arrows and bullets ceased.

A Crow warrior near Zack was strangling, an arrow through his lungs. Owl had an ugly hatchet wound in his left arm. Owl's son lay dead beside his father in the snow. The scalped bodies of the slain were dark blotches on the frozen land below.

The snow had turned crimson in many places, a sanguine hue that became deeper in color as the first rays of the rising sun touched the scene. Such was Christmas morning on the Little Buffalo.

Jeanne had left the bluff. Zack saw her hurrying toward Belzey's lodge. Belzey was unscathed. He had taken toll with two rifles which a squaw had kept reloading for him during the battle. His face was the hue of putty as he gazed around. "Waugh!" he said. "I never seed worse. This child's sick clean down to his moccasins."

Zack spoke to Owl, but the chief did not

answer or look up from the face of his dead son. Zack left him there with his grief and began helping other Crows.

Squaws began to lament their dead, the sadness of their mourning unutterably eerie.

Zack straightened, gazing, a new cold horror driving through him. One of the mourners was Yellow Blossom. She stood before Belzey's lodge bare to the waist in the bitter temperature. She gashed her breast with a knife, sprinkled ashes in her hair, and stood swaying and keening in the dismal dirge of a squaw for a lost son.

Zack began running. Before he could reach the spot Yellow Blossom lifted an ax and chopped off a finger. Zack seized the ax and knife from her hand so that she could do no more damage to herself. Her eyes were fixed in a hypnotic spell of grief.

He pushed past her and stepped into the lodge. Belzey had already arrived. Jeanne stood with Sera, looking at the mountain man who was bending over the pallet on which Hunts-The-Rainbow and their new son lay.

Mother and child were dead. The same Mandan arrow that had transfixed the baby at its mother's breast had driven onward and through Hunts-The-Rainbow's heart.

Belzey did not look up or move. There was the same grief in him that Zack had seen in Owl. And a savage anger.

Jeanne spoke. "How many more are dead?"

"There's nothing that can be done about that now," Zack said. "It's the living who need help."

"Yes," she said. "Yes. Of course."

She and Sera went slowly out to help the Crow women with the wounded. Sera was weeping.

Zack left the village. He picked up the trail of the retreating Mandans and followed it on foot for miles up the creek. At midafternoon, from a high bluff that gave him a view of the plains, he sighted them far away, still heading north. The Mandans had reached their ponies and were riding now. He waited an hour longer to make sure they were not coming back. They vanished into the white glare of the flats, still riding toward the Missouri.

It was long past dark when he returned to the Crow village. The mourning was still going on. The slain Crows had been wrapped in robes and placed on scaffolds. The bodies of the Mandans were being left for the wolves. The lodges were being pulled down and the squaws were packing the parfleche saddle boxes and lashing travois poles on ponies and on dogs. This place would be haunted forever, and the tribe was fleeing from it.

They faced the prospect of traveling in freezing darkness, risking the wrath of the spirits of the night, and of pitching a new temporary camp in the frozen land. It was a place of confusion, with men and squaws in a frenzy of haste.

Zack located Sera amid the turmoil. She was helping Yellow Blossom fell the lodge. He looked around for Jeanne but did not see her.

It was not until the village was on the move with the squaws belaboring the burdened ponies and whining pack dogs that he realized he still had not seen Jeanne. Furthermore it occurred to him that Sera had been avoiding him.

He sought out Sera. "Where is she?" he asked sharply. "Jeanne?"

Sera looked at him, hollow-eyed. "Gone."

"Gone? Where?"

"To Fort Jeanne, of course."

"Not alone?" Zack exclaimed.

"Belzey Williams went with her."

"Why didn't you stop her?" Zack raged.

"I would, if I had known," Sera said. "But she was gone for two hours before I missed her. I thought she was with Floating Leaf. Only Yellow Blossom knew. She told Yellow Blossom to tell you that she will get all these terrible things straightened out when she talks to Paul."

"They'll kill her," Zack rasped. "There is no such person as Paul Chalfant at the post."

Sera stared. Zack did not take the time to explain. He ran to where the pony herd was being hazed along by young Crows. Belzey's two horses, which were all that had been left to him after the Ree raid in the fall, were gone.

He found Owl and explained the situation. "The white girl does not understand that the men she is going to see want her dead in order to protect themselves from white men's law. They have already tried more than once to kill her. They are the ones who led the Mandans. I must get to Fort Jeanne to warn her if you will let me have a good pony."

Owl brought one of his best buffalo ponies and placed the rawhide hackamore thong in Zack's hand. Zack took only the time to borrow a pistol from old Gray Elk to reinforce his rifle. The pistol was a rusty, single-shot weapon, but serviceable. He hastily gulped cold food that Yellow Blossom brought. He borrowed a buffalo robe for additional protection against the cold.

He mounted the pony which was equipped with only a headstall and a surcingle which carried foot loops.

Owl and four mounted Crow warriors, all muffled in blankets and buffalo robes, rode out of the darkness and joined him. They were armed with rifles and bows and arrows.

Accompanying them, sitting lumpily on a pad saddle, was Sera. She too was wrapped in blankets, but beneath that Zack saw that she had at last weakened and changed to breeches for the sake of comfort.

Owl spoke. "There are many people at this Fort Jeanne. You could not fight them all alone, Dark Hair."

Zack, touched, shook hands with the stalwart Crows. "I do not believe I will have to fight all of them," he said in their language. "Not many, I'm sure, will back up the ones I seek."

"If they do," Owl said, "we will walk over their dead bodies to find the ones we want — this Quinn Spain and this Paul

Chalfant who sent the Mandans to slay our sons and brothers."

Owl added grimly, "We may be too late. The Tall Pine is with the white girl. He will send these two to follow the spirit of his son when he finds them."

The Tall Pine was the Crow name for Belzey Williams. Zack had no doubt but that Owl was right. Belzey would have agreed to lead Jeanne over this wintry trail at night for only one reason — to come to close quarters with the men who were responsible for the deaths of Hunts-The-Rainbow and her baby. It was this same thirst for vengeance that burned in Owl and the four warriors. All were mourning dead kin.

Zack looked at Sera and said gently, "You should stay here. This will be a hard trip."

She straightened a little. "I will make it. I won't hold you back. I could never stay here — waiting. You know that. I understand now what you said about Paul Chalfant." She added, "I've ridden horses before. To hounds. But not recently, I must admit." She gave him a challenging look. "You won't have to carry me on your back, fur thief."

Zack pulled his pony alongside, placed

an arm around her, drew her close and kissed her. "You've never been a burden yet," he said. "You're wonderful."

CHAPTER FIFTEEN

Belzey, guiding Jeanne, had followed an Indian trail westward along the Little Buffalo, but the Crows, better acquainted with the terrain, saved many miles of distance by striking directly across country, passing over marshy areas that were impassable normally, but were now hard-frozen.

It was past midnight when they emerged onto the open, snow-covered plains. At times one or the other of the file of riders would snatch his pony to a halt and grab at his rifle, convinced that he had seen enemies rising from the white expanse over which they traveled beneath the chill light of a dying moon. Always it turned out to be a clump of sagebrush, or an illusion of the shadows and of the moonlight, or of the phantoms in the minds of men whose day of battle was not yet ended.

Each time the party would move ahead again, the hooves of the ponies lifting a harsh chorus from the brittle snow.

Not long after daybreak they intersected the tracks of the ponies Jeanne and Belzey were riding. The sign was at least three hours old. Owl said the fort was still a sun's ride away, which Zack estimated as meaning some thirty miles on their tiring ponies. They were still ten to a dozen miles astern in their chase.

They rested the ponies briefly and built a fire for warmth and to heat pemmican. Zack looked at Sera. All during the night journey she had put up a brave front, but he could see now that she was on the verge of collapse.

"You must rest here for a while and come along later in the day," he told her. "One of the Crows will stay with you."

She nodded wearily. "You're right. Above all, I don't want to delay you."

She came to stand for a moment alongside his pony as he mounted. "Will I ever see either of you alive again?" she asked dully. "You? Jeanne?"

Zack bent down and kissed her. "At least you'll be alive, if it comes to that. Stay with the Crows. In the spring they'll see that you get started safely back to St. Louis."

She clung to his hand a moment, then abruptly released it and stepped back. She stood there with the warrior who had been assigned to look after her as Zack and the others rode away.

Zack and the Crows rode in silence

along the plain trail in the snow. At times they slowed the pace to preserve the thinning strength of their mounts.

It was toward noon, and they were moving through a sea of great snow-covered swells in the plains when they encountered more pony tracks. Three riders had entered the trail. These scourings in the snow were a few hours older than the ones that had been made by the mounts of Belzey and the girl.

"These are the white men who were with the Mandans," Owl declared. "These are the ones we will kill."

At the time of the fight, Zack had seen only the two men who had fired at Jeanne. If a third white man had accompanied the Mandans he must have remained under cover during the battle. And he surely must have been Quinn Spain.

Spain probably had found his position precarious with the Mandans who would have been seeking a scapegoat for the disaster that had come upon them at the Crow village. He and his two aides had struck out for the safety of Fort Jeanne. The route they were all following now was a well-beaten trail which Owl said connected the main agency with points on the Powder River to the south. Spain and his crew evidently had passed by early in the day.

As far as Owl and the Crows were concerned, the new tracks in the snow were a satisfying discovery, for it was assurance that the quarry upon whom they sought vengeance was actually within reach. For Zack it only sharpened the sense of urgency and brought almost a panic within him at the impossibility of bridging distance faster.

"The Tall Pine and the white girl may be dead before we reach the fort," he said.

"We do not have wings," Owl said. "We can do no more."

They rode across the white swells. There was no horizon upon which they could depend. It was a land white and dead, where only a frozen tuft of brush or an occasional coulee offered proof that they were making progress. There was no sun in the pale sky, nothing but the glare around them. They pulled robes over their heads, peering from tiny slits as a protection against snow blindness. Even so, Zack was aware of the first burning warning of this affliction. At times he felt sure they were riding in a circle. But the Crows never hesitated. They were certain of their direction — and of their purpose.

Even so, the pursuit seemed hopeless, the handicap of time and distance too great. However, they came upon a site where Belzey and Jeanne had halted and rested their ponies and built a fire. They had remained there for some time, by the tracks in the snow.

Beyond that point the hoofmarks were very fresh. Zack's hopes flamed. Jeanne and Belzey were now less than an hour ahead of them and losing ground. It was evident that their ponies were giving out.

Offsetting that was the fact that Zack's own mount and those of the Crows, while apparently in somewhat better shape, were nearing the end of their endurance.

It was late afternoon when folded hills, bare of snow on the exposed flanks, reared out of the glare ahead. The sun sank low in the sky, the reflection faded, and the world once more had form and contour, ending the eerie sensation of riding through a white mist.

Owl spoke. He informed Zack that the Missouri River was just beyond the low hills. Fort Jeanne was near at hand. They crossed the hills, which proved to be no more than higher swells in the plain. First dusk was hazing the horizon when they came in sight of the frozen Missouri.

Zack began to recognize landmarks. The fort was nearer than he had realized. They descended into the shallow course of a tributary stream and pulled up. The ponies that Belzey and Jeanne had been riding stood picketed where they might have a chance to rustle forage.

The two animals were too exhausted for such effort. They stood huddled together in the bitter temperature, heads drooping. Belzey and Jeanne were afoot.

"We better do the same," Zack exclaimed.

He abandoned his own leg-weary mount and ran ahead for the sake of faster pace. The Crows followed his example.

He came upon a beaten footpath and led the way through thick brush near the river. He suddenly emerged into view of the fort which stood on its bluff less than a quarter of a mile away. Its square log towers and toothed stockade walls stood out against the bleak western sky.

The main gates were closed, but blanket-muffled Indian women were streaming up and down a path that led to a postern entrance, carrying casks and pails of water from the river where holes had been chopped. Smoke was rising from the chimneys where the supper fires were burning.

Belzey, tall and gaunt-faced, stepped into view from cover nearby, a buffalo robe draped from his shoulders. "I knowed you'd make tracks, Zack," he said, "but I didn't figger you'd git here this swift. I'm mighty joyful Owl an' these other men came along, I tell you now."

"Where is Jeanne?" Zack snapped.

Belzey pointed with his rifle. "Up there, I reckon."

"In the fort?" Zack demanded harshly. "You mean you let her go in there alone?"

"She run a high blaze on me," Belzey said. "She sent me away to scout around an' try to find a way to git inside without stirrin' up a hornet's nest. When I come back she was gone. She had slipped away."

"How long ago?"

"I got back jest a few minutes ago," Belzey said. "My fault. I oughtn't to have let her out'n my sight. She still seems to put a lot o' stock in this Uncle of her'n. She told me more'n once as we was on our way that she knew she could straighten things out if she got a chance to talk to Paul Chalfant. That's what she's doin' right now, I reckon."

Zack ran toward the fort, followed by Belzey and the Crows. They sped up the postern path and the women water carriers scrambled out of their way and off into the snow in fear.

Zack raced through the gate into the rear area of the stockade yard. The agent's residence stood at his right.

He ran to it, the others at his heels. Zack crossed the small porch and flung open the door, which was unlocked.

An Indian woman servant screeched and ran across the main room, vanishing through a rear exit. Another door, which opened into the dining room, stood ajar. Through it, Zack saw Jeanne leaping to her feet from a table where she had been seated.

He reached this door, his rifle raised. Quinn Spain also had been at the table. Spain was on his feet. He had seized up a brace of pistols from a sideboard and stood with them cocked.

Spain wore neat green corduroy breeches, a shirt of velvet, and a gray sash and white moccasins. As far as attire went, he was immaculate, but there were the marks of fresh frostbite on his skin and lines of fatigue about his mouth.

Spain's pistols bore on Zack. Perhaps it was Jeanne's shrilly screamed, "No!" More likely it was the fact that Zack also had his hand on the trigger and was ready to fire.

At any rate Spain did not touch off his weapons.

Belzey pushed past Zack. Spain backed away toward an opposite door, keeping the table between them.

Zack looked at the dishes of food on the linen tablecloth. A plate had evidently just been served to Jeanne, for it stood still steaming before the chair in which she had been sitting.

"At least you're still alive," Zack said to her. "You're lucky — and foolish."

She did not answer. She gazed at him, ashen-faced.

Zack spoke to Spain. "Don't move any farther."

Spain maintained his poise. "We were discussing you, Logan," he said. "Miss Fitzhugh told me a very interesting story. We can't tell you how happy we are — and I am referring to everyone at this post — to know that she is alive. And her aunt also. We know the keelboat was destroyed and we had taken it for granted everyone was slaughtered. It was a shocking piece of treachery on the part of the Mandans."

Zack spoke to Belzey. "Shoot him if he moves."

Spain laughed ironically. "You don't really believe Miss Fitzhugh is placing any stock in all the rubbish you've been trying to put in her mind, now do you?"

"How did you know the keelboat was destroyed by Mandans?" Zack asked.

"All the tribes know it," Spain said. "It's common knowledge. Stories like that can't be kept hidden. They carry on the wind. You should know that."

Zack addressed Jeanne without moving his eyes from Spain. "What has he told you?"

"That he had nothing to do with any of the things for which you blame him," she replied.

"And what does your Uncle say?"

"I haven't seen Uncle Paul yet," she said "He's away, visiting some Indian chief."

"I see," Zack said. "A Minitaree, maybe. The same one he was supposed to have been visiting the night Angus Macleod came here to see him."

He spoke to Spain. "You made a fast trip here from the Little Buffalo. You must have pulled in here early this morning."

Spain frowned. "I don't know what you're driving at. The Little Buffalo? What is that supposed to mean? I was up the Missouri a long distance from the Little Buffalo. I went with Paul Chalfant as far as the mouth of the Beaver and stopped at a trapper's camp to see how they were faring. I came back to the fort late last night."

Spain stood slack and apparently sure of himself. He had made no further move toward the opposite door, but he was only a stride from it.

This door apparently opened into another inner room. Zack could not say that he had actually heard any sound from that room, but an instinct kept warning him that someone was there, listening.

He spoke. "And that scar on your face, Spain? I'd say that it looks like someone smashed you with a rifle butt."

Spain's expression did not change. A long, curved scar, newly healed, extended from the corner of his mouth. Zack noticed that at least two of his lower teeth were missing.

"You didn't come here to discuss my personal appearance, Logan," Spain said. "Say your say, and then you and your friends get out."

"You know, of course, that I'm the only thing standing between you and Belzey and Owl," Zack said. "They both lost sons yesterday morning. Belzey lost a wife also. He would kill you fast. Owl would prefer to do it a lot slower."

"Again I tell you I don't know what you're talking about!" Spain exclaimed. He addressed Owl, who stood in the doorway back of Zack with the other three Crows standing at his shoulder. "Your son dead, Owl? Surely, you don't believe I had anything to do with it? You're my friend. All of the Crows are my friends."

Belzey spoke. "Angus Macleod was a friend too."

"And what is that supposed to mean?" Spain countered. But in his manner had come just the faintest change. Zack had seen this in animals he had been stalking. It was the preliminary to the first lunge to spring away.

Zack pushed Jeanne's plate toward him. "Eat," he said.

Jeanne comprehended his meaning. She stared at Zack, horrified. "Surely, you're not trying to say that — that Angus Macleod was poisoned?"

Spain laughed loudly. "That must be it. Ridiculous, isn't it? And he seems to be trying to put the thought in your mind that I am trying to poison you also."

He stepped forward, lifted a fork, and ate from the plate. "Delicious," he said. "But growing cold. You're spoiling our supper, Logan."

Zack had not expected the food to be poisoned. Spain would hardly risk arousing suspicion by repeating such a crime. However, Zack had achieved his purpose. He saw the horror growing in Jeanne. To her and to all of them, Spain's acting was counterfeit. There was no longer any question in Zack's mind but that Belzey had arrived at the truth about the cause of the missionary's death.

"What happened to Paul Chalfant, Spain?" Zack asked.

"Paul? But I just told you. He's visiting —"

"I mean the real Paul Chalfant. Did you murder him too? What did you do with his body?"

The room was completely silent for a moment. "Did you poison him like you poisoned Angus Macleod?" Zack went on. "Who is this man who's posing in Chalfant's place?"

"You're crazy," Spain said, his voice thin.

"You've been milking Fitzhugh Fur for years, Spain," Zack said. "You become too greedy. You knew they were about to get onto you and that you'd lose everything you had stolen and go to prison. You decided that if you could get through this winter, you could pull out early next spring with a final haul and leave the country. Isn't that the way of it?"

"This is all ridiculous," Spain said.

"You murdered Angus Macleod, knowing that if he ever laid eyes on the fake Paul Chalfant, your goose was cooked," Zack went on. "That was the real reason you came upriver to meet him, the day you caught me. Indians, no doubt, had brought word that he was on his way. You wanted to take him under your wing before he reached the fort in order to make sure of what he knew and didn't know. The sables and myself were an unexpected windfall."

Spain's expression was frozen, concealing what might be in his mind.

Zack kept talking. "You had gone in too deep to back out. When you learned that Jeanne Fitzhugh was on her way to Fort Jeanne, you had to go deeper. You had to git rid of her or anyone else who knew the real Paul Chalfant, for the same reason you did away with Angus Macleod. Because, by then, it meant the rope, if you were caught. That's why you led the Mandans on the keelboat. They probably didn't know it was a Fitzhugh boat. You likely told them it was from some other company that was bad medicine to them. You didn't want any witnesses left."

Zack paused a moment, then asked, "Who's in that room back of you, Spain?"

"No one," Spain said.

"It's your fake Paul Chalfant, isn't it?" Zack asked.

Moving with flashing speed, Spain ducked below the table, and dove toward the door. He shouted a warning to someone as he moved. The door was snatched open to permit him to enter and was slammed shut behind him.

Zack leaped at the door but heard the bolt close before his shoulder struck the panel. It did not yield.

He pushed Jeanne into a corner where she would be sheltered. He seized up a heavy chair with which he smashed out a panel in the door.

He hooked an arm through the opening, found the bolt and freed it. No gunfire came, but he could hear the sound of broken glass falling.

He thrust the door open. Belzey came to his side, and they crouched a moment. Zack said, "I'll go in first."

He dove through the opening, rolling aside. Quinn Spain and the thin, graying man, whom Zack had known under the name of Paul Chalfant, were attempting to escape by way of a window at the rear from which they were smashing the glass from the sashes with the muzzles of their pistols.

Spain leveled a weapon. Zack swung up his rifle and fired as he lay on the floor. He knew that he would miss, but hoped to upset Spain's aim. He only partly succeeded. Spain's weapon flamed and Zack felt the slug smash into his left leg.

Spain brought his second pistol to bear and this time there was no way of escape for Zack at that close range. He tried to get at the weapon he had borrowed from Gray Elk, but it was thrust in his belt beneath him.

He tried to roll away, the thought in his mind that he must get to his feet and leap at the man.

But before Spain could pull the trigger a rifle bullet smashed through his body. It was Belzey who had fired. At the same instant an arrow sprouted like an evil growth on Spain's chest. A pace back of Belzey stood Owl, the bow in his hand, the string still vibrating slightly from the power with which the shaft had been propelled.

Spain pitched to the floor and died. Afterwards, in Zack's mind, there was a doubt as to whether it was the bullet or arrow that had slain him. Both, perhaps.

The pseudo Paul Chalfant dropped a

pistol that he held and shrank away from the window. He was gazing in horror at Owl who was nocking another arrow to the string.

Zack tried to get to his feet and found that his wounded leg was useless. He managed to catch Owl's arm, and spoke in the Crow tongue. "Do not kill him. We must talk to this man. There are many things we must learn from him about all of this."

Owl hesitated for a time, then finally lowered the bow. He and Belzey stood looking at Spain's body and all the savagery drained out of them, leaving them very old and very tired.

The thin, gray man pointed to Spain's body. "I'm his brother," he croaked. "He talked me into taking Paul Chalfant's place."

Jeanne came to Zack's side. "You're bleeding," she said, her face almost as gray as that of the false Chalfant.

He cupped her chin in a hand and held her thus, gazing at her. "In all my life I've never been as alive, as sure that I'm going to live to a ripe old age," he said.

She tried to smile, but wept instead. "Yes!" she said. "Oh yes!"

Afterwards, Zack, his leg in splints, lay in

a crowded bedroom in the agent's house and questioned the one who had posed as Paul Chalfant. The man insisted that he really was Quinn Spain's brother. Zack decided that he was telling the truth. There was a faint family resemblance. Zack realized that this was why he had held the impression at their first meeting that he had seen the man in the past.

Sydney Spain, which he gave as his real name, at first denied that he had any knowledge of what had happened to Paul Chalfant.

"You must know," Zack said. "Quit lying, or I'll turn you over to the Crows."

Owl and his warriors were waiting. Sydney Spain looked at them, and the last of his courage crumbled. He began to talk. "Quinn told me that Paul Chalfant was taken down with cholera aboard a steamboat on the Ohio River while he and Quinn were on their way west. All passengers who were sick were carried ashore at a little settlement on the Kentucky shore. Chalfant died there."

"Go on," Zack said.

"My brother told me that he stayed with Chalfant and saw to it that he was buried there, but not under the name of Chalfant. Quinn had got the idea of me taking

Chalfant's place. I was living at a farm-house in the brush on the Illinois shore upriver from St. Louis. The furs that Quinn smuggled out of Fort Jeanne were delivered to me there."

"Who delivered them?"

"A couple of Fitzhugh keelboat captains. They were getting a share of what Quinn stole."

"Are you sure your brother didn't murder Paul Chalfant on that steamboat?" Zack demanded.

"I believe Quinn told the truth about Chalfant dying of cholera," the man pro-tested. "It can be proved, I suppose. I don't remember the name of the settle-ment, but it can be located through the steamboat people, I'm sure. Quinn said Chalfant is buried under the name of Jack Smith."

Zack and Jeanne looked at each other. "Jack Smith," she sighed. "Another of them."

Zack spoke to Sydney Spain. "But your brother turned to murder later on."

"I had no part in those things," the man declared.

"That will be decided by the law," Zack said. "We'll take you back to St. Louis in the spring. We'll want more details from

Zack crouched in hiding in a depression in the snow a dozen feet back from the rim of the rocky ridge which overlooked the village. The tip of the nearest lodge was no more than a pistol shot away.

Owl was concealed a few yards to his left. Belzey was close beside him to the right, so close they could talk in murmurs. Their position commanded the terrain for a considerable distance and there was little danger that a whisper would reach a foe before he approached within sight.

Dug into the snow or crouching back of brush and boulders along the rim were the Crows. They lay huddled in robes and blankets, waiting in silence. Rifles and bows and what sidearms they possessed were being kept warm by their bodies. Particularly sensitive to the cold were the bows, and although the severe weather of the past few days had moderated somewhat Zack estimated that the temperature was still not far above zero.

War axes, hatchets, and clubs lay in the open, along with quivers of arrows. Some of the warriors had knives, and a few owned lances with metal tips. Zack saw at least two of the old-time ivory daggers, formed from walrus tusks which had come down from the north in trade long in the past and had been handed down through the generations. There were two stone-headed war axes, bound with rawhide. Weapons from another age.

The squaws were present also, hidden back of the line of warriors. They too were armed with clubs and hatchets.

Jeanne was with the women. She had no weapon. She had said only one thing to Zack as he and Owl and Belzey were deploying their forces. "I pray to the Almighty that this can be stopped in time."

Zack had placed a hand under her chin, lifted her head and forced her to look at him. "Listen to me," he had said. "These people have fought the Mandans before. They have fought other tribes. They will fight again. You can no more change this than you could stop the wind from blowing, or spare that girl the suffering that brought a baby into this life. Don't try to carry the world on your shoulders. At least this world."

"This is the only world that matters right now," she had responded. "This one that's right around us. This is all wrong, and I feel that I am the cause."

She had left him, drawing her blanket tighter around her. She was pale, her eyes tragic. Beneath the blanket she wore the deerskin smock, leggings, and heavy petti-

you, including the names of these keelboat captains who were in on the trickery. But that can wait awhile."

Many of the clerks and *engagés* at the fort were in the room and had heard Sydney Spain's confession. Zack turned the man over to the senior clerk. "See that he's locked up and kept under guard," he said. "I'll hold you personally responsible."

The two men, who, along with Jules Lebow, had been chiefly instrumental in helping Spain carry out his plans, had fled from the fort when they had learned that Spain was dead.

Some of the *Boisbrûlés* of the fort who had suffered under the domination of Spain's clique, were preparing to take their trail and bring them back, a task that they looked forward to with considerable relish.

"There probably are more rotten apples in the barrel," Zack commented to Jeanne. "But the majority of them seem loyal. The tainted ones can be picked out in the course of time."

"Now, who'd want to talk about rotten apples at a time like this?" A new voice spoke, and Sera came bustling into the room.

She wore her blanket poncho and brought with her the chill memory of the

309

frigid trail over which all of them had traveled from the Crow village. She had determinedly finished the journey to the fort, covering the final miles in darkness, accompanied by her Crow protector.

Jeanne gathered her in her arms, and they wept and laughed and wept again, and kept saying how glad they were that all of them were still alive.

Sera made anxious sounds as she questioned Zack about his injury.

"Leg's busted," Zack said. "I'll be hung up in this blasted bed for days."

"Weeks perhaps," Jeanne said. "Now, let's not be too hasty."

Sera glared around at the staring clerks and Crows. A jug of rum that had been commandeered by the Crows was being passed around.

"Don't you rascals know that this is a sick room!" she thundered. "Clear out of here, every last one of you. And you too, Belzey Williams. You should be getting some rest instead of guzzling liquor. A man at your age ought to know enough to take care of himself."

The assembly departed in a hurry, the Crows whooping a little in defiance, just to show that they weren't entirely cowed by a female.

Belzey paused in the door and pointed a finger at Sera. "You too, ma'am," he said. "Ever hear anybody say three was a crowd?"

Sera went hurrying out with Belzey, carefully closing the door behind her.

Zack and Jeanne listened to their retreating footsteps and to sounds that drifted from the fort yard. The Crows were tipsy on rum and beginning to alternate between howling lamentations for their dead tribesmen in the battle of the Little Buffalo and boastful stomp dancing during which they told of their own valor in that conflict and in the pursuit of Spain.

Jeanne came to sit on the side of the bed. She gazed around the room. The women of the fort had done their best to make Zack comfortable. A fire burned on the hearth. The bed had deep feather mattresses, and the sheets were gleaming white, the quilts the colorful handiwork of clever French-Indian wives.

"It's more cheerful than the Owl's Nest," she said. She looked down at him. "But I will never forget the nest. I want to go back there — often."

He reached out and drew her down, so that her face was against his.

"You'll have company," he said. "Wherever you go."

"That is good," she sighed. "I would not go there without the fur thief, that great bear of a man who once lived there and compelled me to fall in love with him."